The Day of
the Jackal

FREDERICK FORSYTH

Level 4

Retold by John Escott
Series Editors: Andy Hopkins and Jocelyn Potter

Pearson Education Limited
Edinburgh Gate, Harlow,
Essex CM20 2JE, England
and Associated Companies throughout the world.

ISBN: 978-1-4058-8210-1

First published in Great Britain by Hutchinson (& Co.) Publishers Ltd 1971
First published by Penguin Books Ltd 1999
This edition published 2008

3 5 7 9 10 8 6 4 2

Original copyright © Frederick Forsyth 1971
Text copyright © Pearson Education Ltd 2008
Illustrations copyright © Ron Tiner 1999

The moral rights of the authors have been asserted

Typeset by Graphicraft Ltd, Hong Kong
Set in 11/14pt Bembo
Printed in China
SWTC/02

Published by Pearson Education Ltd in association with
Penguin Books Ltd, both companies being subsidiaries of Pearson Plc

For a complete list of the titles available in the Penguin Readers series please write to your local
Pearson Longman office or to: Penguin Readers Marketing Department, Pearson Education,
Edinburgh Gate, Harlow, Essex CM20 2JE, England.

Contents

Introduction

A minute later, the Jackal saw a tall figure in a grey suit, with the familiar head and nose, in the back of the first car as it went past.

'The next time I see your face,' he silently told the figure in the car, 'it will be at the end of a rifle.'

'The Jackal' is a professional killer who has been hired to kill Charles de Gaulle, the President of France. This exciting story follows the killer's careful planning and preparations for the assassination – as police detective Claude Lebel tries to stop him, and to save the president's life.

Frederick Forsyth, the writer of this story, was born in 1938. When he left school he attended the University of Granada in Spain. From 1956 to 1958 he did his National Service in the Royal Air Force, where he became a pilot. After this he worked for a local newspaper before becoming an international news reporter. From 1961 to 1965 he worked for Reuters, the news organisation, and his job took him to London, Paris and East Berlin. He also worked for several years as a radio and television reporter for the BBC.

From July to September 1967 he reported on the Biafran war in Nigeria. When he left the BBC, he returned independently to Biafra and continued to report on the situation there. In 1969, he wrote a book about the war called *The Biafra Story*. He then decided to write a work of fiction. He had read many adventure stories but felt that few writers knew much about their subjects. So he used his experience and knowledge from his work as a journalist. The result was *The Day of the Jackal*. It appeared in 1971, became an international success and was translated into thirty languages. In 1973 it was made into a popular film with the same name.

Although the story is fictional, most of the characters are real, but names and descriptions were changed. One character with his real name is of course Charles de Gaulle. A number of people really did try to assassinate him in the early 1960s.

De Gaulle was born in 1890 and as a young man became an officer in the French army. He fought in the First World War, where he was almost killed, and was taken prisoner. His later views on modern war made him unpopular with the French generals. But when the German army entered France in 1940, de Gaulle's soldiers had one of the few successes against them. When France stopped fighting in June 1940, he refused to accept this. He flew to London, and on 18th June he broadcast to the French people, asking them to continue to fight the Germans. Although very few French people heard the broadcast, it later became famous. The final chapter of *The Day of the Jackal* takes place mainly in a square called the Place du 18 juin (of 18th June).

De Gaulle then organised French people outside France into the Free French forces, and thousands of them joined the soldiers from Britain and other countries who landed in Normandy, in the north of France, in June 1944. When the soldiers later came close to Paris, they stopped because they were afraid that the city would be destroyed. But the people of Paris had begun to fight and de Gaulle was worried that the Germans would kill them. He said he would take the Free French into the city alone if necessary. It was agreed that Paris should be freed immediately, and de Gaulle's men led the attack on the city. The Germans stopped fighting there on 25th August and this became known as Liberation Day. It plays an important part in this story.

Members of a secret organisation, the OAS, were the people who tried to kill de Gaulle in the 1960s. Most were French people who lived in Algeria. At the time, Algeria was ruled by France, but its neighbours Morocco and Tunisia had recently become independent. Algeria was different, though, because over a million French people lived there. Most had been born in the country but they still thought of themselves as French. In May 1958, to keep the country under French control, they took the government buildings, supported by French soldiers in Algeria.

For some years, the Algerian people had fought against French rule. De Gaulle, as president, felt that the French could win but that other countries would not accept this. So he prepared the way for Algerian independence, and this happened in July 1962. Because of this, most of the French people in Algeria moved to France. On 22nd August a number of OAS men fired at de Gaulle's car with machine guns. Although twelve bullets hit the car, de Gaulle and his wife were unhurt. This event is described in the first chapter of the book, but then the story moves from fact into fiction. The leader of the OAS, Colonel Marc Rodin, makes a new plan . . . and the Jackal is hired.

The book took only thirty-five days to write, but Forsyth had begun to plan the story in 1962–63 when he worked in Paris. Because of his work as a reporter, he was able to talk to many people who were part of the similar real-life situation. These included de Gaulle's bodyguards and drivers, a gun maker and even a professional assassin. Before the book appeared, it was read by André Malraux, one of de Gaulle's government ministers.

The Day of the Jackal is Frederick Forsyth's most popular book, but he has written many others. The stories are often told against a background of real events, people and places, taken from his own experiences. His books have sold more than 50 million copies around the world.

CHAPTER 1

The Jackal

It was 7.53 on the evening of 22nd August 1962 when Colonel Jean-Marie Bastien-Thiry of the Secret Army Organisation (or OAS) received the telephone call he was expecting. He was in a café in Meudon, just outside Paris. He listened for a few moments before saying goodbye, then he walked out of the café and took a newspaper from under his arm. Carefully, he opened and closed it twice. Across the street a young woman turned from the window of her flat towards the twelve men who were sitting in her room.

'It's road number two,' she said.

The men went down the stairs at the back of the building and into a narrow street where six vehicles were waiting.

It was 7.55.

The car carrying President Charles de Gaulle and his wife was travelling out of the centre of Paris. After leaving most of the traffic behind, the driver increased the speed of the long black DS 19 Citroën. The two motorcycle riders who were beside the car dropped back behind it.

It was 8.18 when Bastien-Thiry saw the car and the motorcycles coming towards him down the Avenue de la Libération. Quickly, he turned and waved his newspaper at the men who were further down the road on the opposite side. Unfortunately, the evening light was darker than Bastien-Thiry had expected, and the men could not see him waving.

It was a serious mistake.

'Has the Colonel waved his paper yet?' one of them asked.

As he was talking, the President's car appeared in front of him. It was moving fast.

'Shoot!' he shouted to the other men.

But they were already too late. Only twelve bullets hit the President's car, and most of those hit the back of it. Nobody inside was hurt.

A second group of OAS men were waiting in a car in the Avenue de Bois, a side road off the Avenue de la Libération. They had expected the first group to force the President's car to stop, and were surprised to see it travelling fast towards them. There was nothing they could do. Seconds later, the long black Citroën was gone.

They, like others before them, had failed to assassinate the President of France.

♦

In the middle of June 1963, three OAS men were meeting in room 64 of the Hotel Kleist, in Vienna. Colonel Marc Rodin was sitting at the desk and talking. The other two men – René Montclair and André Casson – were looking uncomfortable.

'Twice in the past four months we nearly killed de Gaulle,' Rodin was saying. 'Both times we failed because of simple, stupid mistakes. The same kind of mistakes that allowed the police to catch Bastien-Thiry.'

He hated de Gaulle. Like a lot of people in France he thought the President had been wrong to make Algeria independent. But while most were happy just to complain about it, Rodin and some others from the army had formed an action group. They called themselves the OAS, and their main purpose was to kill the President.

'All right, all right. What do you suggest?' asked Montclair.

'I believe there is only one way to be certain of success,' said Rodin. 'We must accept that all those we know who are able to do the job are also known to the secret police. So, gentlemen, we must use an outsider. A foreigner. He will not be a member of the

Only twelve bullets hit the President's car ...

OAS. No policeman in France will know him, and he will not be on any file. He will travel with a foreign passport, do the job, and go back to his own country.'

'A professional assassin,' said Montclair.

'Exactly,' replied Rodin. 'A man who will not do the job for love of us, or for France – who will only work for money. A lot of money.'

'How can we find a man like that?' asked Casson.

'First things first, gentlemen,' said Rodin. 'Do you agree with the idea?'

Montclair and Casson looked at each other, then turned to Rodin. 'We agree,' they said.

'There are men and women in the OAS who report our plans to the secret police,' said Rodin. 'We know that, so our plans must be a secret. Now, I asked the two of you to come here because I am certain you can keep a secret, and because I need your help. We will be responsible for every detail.' He put three files on the desk. 'Study these, and then we will talk.'

Casson and Montclair began to read. When they had exchanged and finished all three, Rodin looked at them.

'For the moment, we will call them the German, the South African and the Englishman,' he said. 'André?'

'The Englishman,' said Casson.

'René?' asked Rodin.

'I agree,' replied Montclair.

'Are you sure about him?' Casson asked Rodin. He pointed at the file. 'Did he really kill those men?'

'I was surprised myself,' said Rodin. 'I spent a lot of time on this one, and checked as far as it's possible to check. For this kind of job, he has all the advantages except one.'

'What's that?' asked Montclair quickly.

'He will not be cheap. How is the financial situation, René?'

'Not very good,' said Montclair.

'Then we have to get some money from somewhere,' said Rodin. 'But first we must find out how much we will need.'

'Which means that we must ask the Englishman if he will do the job, and how much it will cost,' said Casson.

Rodin looked at his watch. 'It's just after one o'clock. The Englishman could fly to Vienna tonight on the evening plane, and we could meet him here after dinner. I will telephone my man in London and try to organise it.'

♦

That evening, a tall, fair-haired Englishman entered the Hotel Kleist and walked confidently up the stairs. At the top, he stopped and looked carefully along the narrow hall. He could see room 64, but he could also see a curtain opposite the room, and the toe of one black shoe showing below it.

The Englishman turned and walked back downstairs to the hotel desk. 'The telephone, please,' he said to the man behind the desk. 'And connect me to room 64.'

After a moment or two, he was connected.

'Get that man out from behind that curtain in fifteen seconds, or I am going back home,' he said, and put the telephone down. Then he walked back up the stairs.

As he reached the top, the door of room 64 opened. Colonel Rodin came out. The Colonel looked down the hall at the Englishman, then called softly, 'Viktor.' The curtain moved, and a large man appeared. 'It's all right, Viktor,' said Rodin. 'He is expected.'

Viktor Kowalski watched silently as the Englishman walked along the hall and entered room 64.

Casson and Montclair were waiting inside. They looked at their visitor and saw a tall, fit man in his thirties. The sight pleased them, but they also noticed that his eyes were cold and dangerous.

'Let me introduce myself,' said Rodin. 'I am Colonel –'

'I know,' said the Englishman. 'You are Colonel Marc Rodin, chief of operations of the OAS. You are René Montclair, and you are André Casson.'

'You seem to know a lot already,' said Casson.

'Gentlemen, let us be honest,' said the Englishman. 'I know what you are, and you know what I am. We all have unusual jobs. You are hunted, but I am free to move around. You've been asking questions about me, I know that. I have learnt all I need to know about your organisation from French newspaper files. But what do you want?'

Casson and Montclair waited for the Colonel to speak first. Rodin and the Englishman looked at each other in silence for several moments, then Rodin said, 'Our supporters have tried on six occasions to assassinate de Gaulle. Four times the plans were discovered in the early stages. Twice they simply failed. We are now thinking about hiring a professional to do the job. But what do you think? Is it possible to kill him?'

'Of course it's possible to kill him,' said the Englishman. 'It is escaping afterwards that will be extremely difficult. All important men have people to protect them, but the guards become lazy when nothing happens for a long time. Then it's easy for a professional to fire an unexpected bullet and escape. But the men who protect de Gaulle know that the OAS want him dead, and they are ready and waiting for someone else to try. If it happens, they will immediately go after the assassin. It can be done, gentlemen, but it will be one of the most difficult jobs in the world at the moment.'

'Will you do it?' asked Rodin quietly.

'Yes,' said the Englishman, 'but it will cost a lot of money. You must understand that the man who does this will never work again. It will be too dangerous.'

'How much?' asked Montclair.

'Half a million dollars. Cash. Two hundred and fifty thousand before I begin, and two hundred and fifty thousand when I complete the job.'

Montclair jumped out of his chair. 'Half a million dollars!' he shouted. 'You are crazy!'

'No,' replied the Englishman calmly. 'But I am the best.'

'We do not have half a million dollars in cash,' said Rodin.

'I know that,' said the Englishman. 'You will have to get it from somewhere, if you want the job done. But if I'm too expensive —' He started to get out of his chair.

'Sit down,' said Rodin. 'We'll get the money.'

'Good,' said the Englishman. 'How many people in your organisation know of your idea to hire an assassin?'

'Only the three of us in this room,' replied Rodin.

'Good,' said the Englishman. 'Nobody else must know. I shall make my own plans. You will not know the details, and you will not hear from me again. I shall leave you the name of my bank in Switzerland. They will tell me when the first two hundred and fifty thousand dollars are in my account.'

'All right,' said Rodin. 'But we have men in France who can help you with information. Some hold important government positions.'

'Fine,' said the Englishman, after a moment. 'When you're ready, send me a single telephone number. A Paris number that I can ring from anywhere in France. But the man on the end of the telephone must not know what I am doing.'

'But how can we get the money?' Montclair wanted to know.

'Use your organisation to rob a few banks,' suggested the Englishman, coldly.

'One last thing,' said Rodin. 'Your name. Clearly you do not want to give us your real name. So what shall we call you?'

The Englishman thought for a moment. 'The Jackal,' he said. 'Will that be all right?'

'The Jackal. Yes,' said Rodin. 'I like it.'

He took the Englishman to the door and opened it. Viktor Kowalski appeared from behind the curtain. Rodin smiled for the first time and shook the Englishman's hand. 'You will begin planning soon?' he asked. 'We do not want to lose any time, do we? Good. Then good night, Mr Jackal.'

♦

During the second half of June and the whole of July in 1963, banks and jewellers' shops were robbed all over France. It did not take the French government long to realise that the OAS were responsible for these crimes. Or that the OAS needed money quickly for some reason.

In London, the Jackal was making careful plans and reading everything he could find about or by General de Gaulle. The main question in his mind was: 'Where, when and how shall I do it?' He was reading a 1962 French newspaper when the answer to 'when' and 'where' came to him. Suddenly, he realised that there was one day every year on which Charles de Gaulle always appeared in public. It took many more hours of thought before he was able to decide *how* he was going to kill de Gaulle.

♦

The passengers began to leave the plane from Copenhagen at London's Heathrow Airport. The Jackal watched them through the window of the airport building. The eighth passenger to step out of the plane was a priest. He was about fifty years old and had grey hair. Like the Jackal, he was tall with wide shoulders.

Fifteen minutes later, the priest appeared from the Customs hall and went to one of the banks to change some money. He then took a taxi into the centre of London.

He did not notice the fair-haired Englishman following in the car behind. And he did not see him later, sitting in the entrance

Rodin smiled for the first time . . .

hall of the hotel where he was staying. That evening, the priest gave his room key to the man behind the desk and went into the hotel restaurant.

The Jackal noticed that the key was for room 47.

He waited until the priest was in the restaurant, then went upstairs to room 47. Using a small knife, he carefully opened the lock on the door and went inside. The priest's passport was on the table beside the bed. The Jackal took it and was out in the hall again in seconds.

Two days later Marty Schulberg, an American student, arrived at Heathrow Airport from New York. He was twenty-five years old, had brown hair and was wearing glasses. He went to the American Express* office to change some travellers' cheques, then put the money and his passport into a small bag. A few minutes later, he put the bag down while he tried to find a taxi. Three seconds later it was gone.

That evening, the Jackal studied the faces on the passports of the two men – the Danish priest and the young American student. It took him a whole day and visits to a number of different shops to get the clothes, glasses and wigs that he needed.

Next, he wanted a false British passport.

Alexander Duggan was born on 3rd April 1929 and died on 8th November 1931. The Jackal discovered this in the church records of a small country town. He then requested and received Alexander Duggan's birth and death certificates from the Office of Births, Marriages and Deaths in London. He got a passport form and filled it in using the name Alexander Duggan. Then he sent the form and the birth certificate to the Passport Office, and burnt the death certificate. Four days later, his new passport arrived.

And the next day, the Jackal flew to Brussels.

* American Express: a company that sells travel and financial services through its offices around the world.

CHAPTER 2

A Very Special Gun

The tall, fair-haired English visitor that Paul Goossens had been waiting for arrived at midday. Goossens, a short older man, took him into his small but excellent workshop.

'How can I help you?' asked the Belgian.

'I believe my friend Louis telephoned you about me earlier,' said the Englishman. 'Did he tell you what my business is?'

'No,' replied Goossens. 'Only that you needed a gun, and that you would pay for it in cash, in English money.'

'A very special gun, for a very special job,' said the Englishman. He explained the nature of his work without telling the Belgian who he planned to kill. 'I need a rifle which can be put together and taken to pieces,' he continued, 'and which will fit into a narrow metal tube.' He described in more detail exactly what he wanted.

The gun-maker looked both interested and excited as he listened. 'Not an easy job in a small workshop, but possible,' he said when the Englishman had finished. 'Will you be aiming at the head or the chest?'

'It will probably have to be the head. I may get a shot at the chest, but the head is surer.'

'Surer to kill, yes, if you get a good hit,' said the Belgian. 'But you sound uncertain about this. Do you expect someone to pass by and perhaps get in the way?'

'Perhaps,' replied the Englishman.

'Will the . . . er . . . gentleman move slowly, fast or not at all?' asked Goossens.

'Not at all,' said the Englishman.

'You spoke about a metal tube for carrying the gun. What are you thinking of, exactly?'

The Englishman put a hand inside his coat, and for a second there was fear in the smaller man's eyes. But the Englishman only took a silver pencil from his pocket. He drew something on one of the pieces of paper on Goossens's desk.

'Do you recognise that?' he asked.

'Of course,' replied the Belgian.

'It is made of several empty tubes which fit together. The rifle will go inside. The shoulder-rest of the rifle is this part . . . here . . . complete. It is the only piece which serves two purposes and will not change in any way.'

The little Belgian looked at the drawing for several seconds, then he said, 'It is very clever. But so simple. I shall do it.'

The Englishman showed no emotion. 'Good,' he said. 'I shall need the gun in fourteen days. Can that be done?'

'Yes,' replied Goossens. 'But perhaps it would be better if you came back in twelve days. I may need to discuss some last-minute details with you. Can you do that?'

'Yes, any time between seven and fourteen days from now. But I must be back in London by 4th August,' said the Englishman. 'Now, how much will it cost?'

The Belgian thought for a while. 'One thousand English pounds,' he said at last. 'It is not a simple rifle, and I believe I am the only man in Europe who can make a perfect job of it. Then there will be bullets and other materials . . . another two hundred pounds.'

'Agreed,' said the Englishman without argument. He took five hundred pounds from his pocket and gave it to the other man. 'I will bring you the other seven hundred when I return in twelve days.'

The Belgian quickly put the money into his pocket. 'It is a pleasure to do business with a professional and a gentleman,' he said.

'One more thing,' continued his visitor. 'You will not try to speak to Louis, or ask him or anyone else who I am. If you do, I shall hear about it . . . and you will die. Is that understood?'

Paul Goossens faced many dangerous men who came to ask him for special or unusual guns, but there was something particularly cold and frightening about the visitor from England.

'I do not want to know anything about you,' he said quietly. 'And the gun you will receive will have no number, no mark of any kind. It is important to me too that nothing you do can ever be connected with me.'

◆

The Jackal walked out into the bright sunshine of the Brussels street, where he took a taxi into the city centre. He found the man he was looking for in a bar off the Rue Neuve. Once again, his friend Louis had organised the appointment.

The two men took their drinks to a quiet table in a corner of the room, then the Jackal took out his driving certificate, which was in his own name.

'This,' he told the Belgian, 'belonged to a man who is now dead. As I am not allowed to drive in Britain, I need a new front page in my own name.' And he put the passport in the name of Duggan in front of the forger.

The man opposite looked at the passport first, noticing that it was new, and then looked carefully at the Englishman. He studied the driving certificate for a few more minutes. 'Not difficult,' he said. 'Is that all you want?'

'No, there are two other papers.' The Jackal described them in detail.

The Belgian's eyes narrowed in thought. 'That is not so easy. The French identity card, OK. But the other one . . . that is a most unusual request. And the photograph will not be easy. You say there must be a difference in age, in hair colouring and length. It will take some time. How long can you stay in Brussels?'

'Not long,' said the Jackal. 'I could be back on 1st August, but I have to return to London on 4th August.'

The Belgian looked long and hard at the photograph in the passport. Then he copied the name Alexander James Quentin Duggan on to some paper. He put this and the driving certificate in his pocket, and he passed the photograph back to the Jackal. 'It will take time,' he said. 'And money.'

'How much?' asked the Jackal.

'One hundred and fifty English pounds,' said the forger.

'All right. I'll pay you a hundred pounds now, and the rest when you deliver the documents,' said the Jackal.

The Belgian stood up. 'Then let's take the photographs.'

They took a taxi to a small shop a mile away, where there were a few photographs of babies and wedding groups in the window. The Belgian led the Jackal down some steps beside the shop to a door. He unlocked this, then took his guest into the room inside.

There was a large box in one corner, and in it were a variety of expensive cameras, as well as wigs, false beards and glasses. It took two hours to take the necessary photographs, and after an hour the Belgian went to the box and took out a grey wig.

'Do you think your own hair, cut to this length and coloured grey, could look like this?' asked the forger.

The Jackal examined the wig. 'We can try it, and see how it looks in the photograph.'

It was successful. Later, after the Belgian had worked on the Jackal's face and hair and had produced prints of the photographs, they examined the picture of a tired, fifty-year-old man with grey hair and grey skin.

'I think it will work,' said the Belgian. 'It will be a very small picture on the identity card. The important thing is your hair. It must be cut and coloured grey, perhaps even greyer than in the photograph. And your skin must be grey too, like an old man's.'

'I think it will work.'

He explained how to do this while the Jackal listened carefully.

The Jackal took a hundred pounds from his pocket and gave it to the forger. 'How do I communicate with you? Shall I come here?'

The Belgian thought for a minute. 'No. I shall wait from six until seven each evening in the bar where we met tonight, on each of the first three days of August.'

The Englishman took off the wig and washed his face. Then he turned to the Belgian.

'There are certain things I want to make clear. When you have finished the job you will return to me the new driving certificate, and the page from the one you have now. You will also give me all the negatives and prints of the photographs we have just taken. You will forget the names of Duggan and of the first owner of that driving certificate. You may choose a name for the two French documents you are going to produce. After giving them to me, you will forget those names also. You will never speak of this job again. If you do not do the things I am telling you, you will die. Do you understand?'

The Belgian looked at him. For the first time he realised that this was no ordinary customer. 'Yes,' he replied.

Seconds later the Englishman was gone into the night.

And the next morning he caught a fast train to Paris.

It was 22nd July.

♦

On that same morning, Colonel Rolland of the French secret service sat at his desk and looked at the two pieces of paper in front of him. The first was a report from their office in Rome, saying that Rodin, Montclair and Casson were still in their hotel rooms, guarded by their eight guards. They had not moved out of there since their arrival on 18th June.

He opened the file on the right of his desk, and read through the Rome report of 30th June until he found the sentence that he wanted. Each day, it said, one of the guards left the hotel and walked to the post office to collect the mail. The guard was known to be Viktor Kowalski.

Colonel Rolland now looked at the second of the two reports that had come in that morning. It was from the Metz police, stating that a man had been questioned in a bar, and had half-killed two policemen in a fight. Later it was discovered that he was Sandor Kovacs, a Hungarian who was also a member of the OAS and who was wanted for several murders in Algeria during 1961. His partner at that time was another OAS gunman, Viktor Kowalski, who was still free. End of message.

Rolland finished reading the report and, after a moment, asked his secretary for the file on Viktor Kowalski. It arrived ten minutes later. He spent the next hour reading it, and then made a decision. With the help of others, including one person who would not be happy to help, he was going to write a letter.

◆

The Jackal spent five days walking round several famous places in Paris, including the Arc de Triomphe and the great church of Notre Dame. But his last visit was to the square known as the Place du 18 juin 1940, at the southern end of the Rue de Rennes. It was 28th July.

He looked round at the tall, narrow-fronted buildings on each side of the Rue de Rennes that also looked over the square. Slowly he walked round the square to the southern side and turned to look back down the street. He was sure that the President of France would come, one last time, on a certain day – the day that the Jackal had chosen.

The distance from the top floor of the corner house on the western side of the Rue de Rennes to the centre of the square was about one hundred and thirty metres. Both corner houses on the street where it met the square were suitable. The first three buildings were possible choices, but after them it became too difficult.

The Jackal decided to study the three corner buildings on the western side first, and walked over to a café on the eastern corner. He ordered a coffee and looked at the three buildings across the street. He stayed for three hours.

The next day he was back again. It would be the middle of the afternoon on the day that he expected to fire the rifle, so he waited until four o'clock in the afternoon. He noticed that the top windows of two houses on the west side of the street were getting only a little sunlight, while the sun still burned brightly into the top windows of the houses on the eastern side.

The next day he noticed the woman who looked after the flats in one of the buildings, and heard a waiter in a café call her Madame Berthe. She was a cheerful, grandmotherly woman who said 'Good morning!' to the people who entered or left her building. Just before four o'clock she went down the road to the baker's shop.

The Jackal quickly entered the building and ran up the stairs. On the sixth floor there were two doors to flats which had windows looking over the square. These were the windows he had been watching for so long from the street below. He listened for a moment but there was no sound from either flat. He examined the locks on the doors. Both were strong, and he realised that he would need keys. Madame Berthe would certainly have one for each flat somewhere in her room downstairs.

A few minutes later he was running softly down the stairs again. He had been in the building less than five minutes. Madame Berthe was back. He saw her through the clouded glass window in the door of her little room. Moments later, he was outside.

He turned left up the Rue de Rennes and walked past two other buildings, then the front of a post office. At the corner of the building was a narrow street, the Rue Littre. He turned into it, still following the wall of the post office. Where the building ended there was a narrow, covered path which led into a small sunlit square. On the far side of the little square he could see the bottom steps of the fire escape of the building he had just left. He smiled. He had found his way to escape.

At the end of the Rue Littre he turned into a side road and walked back to where it joined the main road. He was looking for a taxi when a policeman went by on a motorcycle. The policeman stopped all the traffic coming out of the side road, as well as that going down the main road. The cars coming up the main road were directed on to the right-hand side of the road.

The Jackal saw two more police motorcycles coming towards him. They were followed by two Citroën DS 19s. A minute later, the Jackal saw a tall figure in a grey suit, with the familiar head and nose, in the back of the first car as it went past.

'The next time I see your face,' he silently told the figure in the car, 'it will be at the end of a rifle.'

♦

On the last day of the month, the Jackal was busy. He spent the morning at a market, where he bought a flat black hat, a pair of old shoes, some not-very-clean trousers, and a very long army coat which covered his knees. He also bought several old medals.

He then collected his luggage from his hotel and caught a train to Brussels, arriving there in the last hours of July.

CHAPTER 3

A Trip to the Forest

The letter for Viktor Kowalski arrived in Rome the following morning. He was surprised to see that it was from Kovacs, a man he had not seen for a year.

Kovacs wrote that he had read in a newspaper that Rodin, Montclair and Casson were hiding at the hotel in Rome. He had guessed that his old friend would be with them. He then told Viktor that things were getting difficult in France; the police kept asking for identity papers, and orders were still coming through for robbing jewellers. Kovacs said that he had robbed four of these, and it was no fun, especially when they had to pass on the money to the organisation.

The last part of the letter informed Viktor that Kovacs had met Michel some weeks before. Michel had been talking to JoJo, and JoJo had said little Sylvie was sick. She had something seriously wrong with her blood, and he, Kovacs, hoped that she would soon be all right. He told Viktor not to worry.

But Viktor did worry. Sylvie was his daughter.

Sylvie's mother was a woman Viktor had first met in Marseilles, in a bar, in 1955. Some time later, she had told Viktor that she was expecting his child. 'But I'm not going to have it,' she said. Viktor had hit her — hard. 'If you don't have it, I'll kill you,' he had told her. So the baby had been born and Viktor had found a Polish friend, Josef Grzybowski (known as JoJo), and his wife who agreed to take the blue-eyed, golden-haired little girl and look after her as their own daughter. They had named her Sylvie.

Viktor had only seen his daughter twice in his life. The first time Sylvie had been two, the next time four and a half. The little girl liked her big Uncle Viktor, who brought her presents, but he never spoke about her to anyone else.

But he did complete the necessary document to make sure that everything he owned went to the girl when he died, and a copy of this document was passed to Colonel Rolland of the French secret service and was now in Kowalski's file in Rolland's office.

Viktor worried about Sylvie for the rest of the morning.

♦

A letter in the afternoon mail brought Rodin the good news that the OAS bank accounts in Switzerland now contained over two hundred and fifty thousand dollars.

♦

On the morning that Kowalski received his letter, the Jackal left his hotel in Brussels and took a taxi to the corner of the street where Paul Goossens lived. He arrived at 10.30 and spent half an hour watching everything from behind a newspaper as he sat on a seat in the public gardens at the end of the street.

It seemed quiet, and at eleven o'clock he went to Goossens's house. The gun-maker opened the door and led him to the little office off the hall, then carefully locked the front door.

Minutes later, the Jackal was examining the rifle. After a while, he turned to the Belgian, satisfied. 'Good,' he said. 'Very good. A beautiful piece of work.'

The Belgian reached into the drawer of his desk and pulled out a box of a hundred bullets. The box had been opened and six were missing.

'These are for practice,' said Goossens. 'I have taken six out to make bullets with explosive ends.'

'These are for practice.'

The Jackal knew about explosive bullets, although he had never used them. They caused an explosion like a small bomb when they hit a human body.

Goossens showed one of the special bullets to the Jackal.

'They look all right to me,' said the assassin. 'Now, the tubes?'

'They have been more difficult,' said Goossens. 'To keep them as narrow as possible, I bought very thin metal. But it bent too easily. The new metal I have now takes longer to work with. I began yesterday —'

'All right,' said the Jackal. 'But I need them, and I need them perfect. When will they be ready?'

'It is difficult to say,' said the Belgian. 'Five, six days, a week perhaps . . .'

The Englishman showed no sign that he was annoyed. 'All right,' he said. 'It will mean I have to change my travel plans, but perhaps that won't be too serious. And I'll take the rifle now. I want to test it, so I shall need some of the ordinary bullets, and one of the explosive ones. I shall also need somewhere quiet and secret to practise. Where do you suggest?'

Goossens thought for a moment. 'In the forest of the Ardennes,' he said at last. 'You could be there and back in a day. Today is Thursday, the weekend starts tomorrow and the forest might be too full of people walking. I would suggest Monday the 5th. I hope to have the job finished by Tuesday or Wednesday.'

The Englishman paid the gun-maker another five hundred pounds before he left to go back to his hotel.

He met the forger in the bar near the Rue Neuve that evening. 'Finished?' he asked.

'Yes, all finished,' replied the forger.

The Englishman held out his hand. 'Show me.'

The Belgian lit a cigarette. 'This is a very public place,' he said. 'Also you need good light to examine them. They are at my shop.'

The Jackal looked at him coldly for a moment, then said, 'All right. We'll go and have a look at them in private.'

The forger led the way to his photographer's shop. Inside, he pulled a flat brown envelope from his pocket and took out three cards. He put them down on a table, under the light.

The Englishman picked up the first of the three cards. It was his driving certificate, now in the name of Alexander James Quentin Duggan. It was a perfect forgery. The second card was a French identity card in the name of André Martin, aged fifty-three, living in Paris. His own photograph was in a corner of the card. He looked twenty years older and had grey hair.

The third card interested him most. The photograph was slightly different from the one on the identity card. It was another picture of himself that had been taken nearly two weeks earlier, but the shirt seemed to be darker and there was just the suggestion of a beard round the chin. Two different photographs of the same man, which seemed to have been taken at different times and in different clothes. Both were excellent forgeries.

'Very nice,' said the Jackal, putting the cards into his pocket. 'You want another fifty pounds, I think.' He took ten five-pound notes from his pocket and gave them to the forger. Before he let go of them, the Jackal said, 'I believe there is something more.'

'Something more?' said the Belgian.

'The real front page of the driving certificate,' said the Jackal. 'I want it back.'

The forger let go of the money and turned away. 'I thought we might be able to have a little talk about that piece of paper.'

'Yes?' The Jackal's eyes were without expression.

'The real front page of the driving certificate with, I imagine, your real name on it, is not here. It is in a very safe place. You see, in my business I have to be very careful —'

'What do you want?' asked the Jackal.

'A little more than the hundred and fifty pounds we spoke of in this room,' said the Belgian. 'I also have the negatives of the photographs which I took of you, and another picture of you which I took when you were not looking, when you were standing under the lights. Now I'm sure you would find it most inconvenient if these documents reached the hands of the British and French police –'

'How much?' said the Jackal.

'One thousand pounds,' said the forger.

'All right,' said the Englishman. 'I can have the thousand pounds by midday tomorrow. But we do not meet here.'

The forger was surprised. 'But it is very quiet, very private. People only come here if they are invited by me. I have to be very careful. Some of the pictures I take here...' He smiled. 'Well, they are not – what shall I say? – for children's eyes.'

The Englishman started to laugh. The Belgian laughed with him, sharing the joke. Then the Englishman put his hands on the other man's arms and held him tightly. The Belgian was still laughing when the Jackal pushed his knee into the forger's lower stomach – hard! The forger shouted with pain and the Jackal allowed him to fall on to the floor on his knees.

Then he broke the forger's neck.

He found some keys in the dead man's pocket. The fourth key that he tried opened the large box in the corner. He spent ten minutes emptying it of clothes and wigs. When it was empty, he lifted the dead man's body into the box, and put the other things back in on top of it. Then he locked the box again.

He sat down and lit a cigarette. He planned to wait until it was dark outside before leaving.

The Jackal decided that it would probably be some time before the body was found. If the forger did not appear for a little while, his friends would probably think he had gone out of town. And it would almost certainly be some months before anyone discovered the forger's 'safe place'.

The Jackal left the shop at 9.30 that evening, locking the door behind him. No one passed him as he went down the street.

The next day, Friday, he went shopping. He bought a string shopping bag, a hunting knife, a can of pink paint and a can of brown, and two thin paint brushes.

Back at the hotel, he used his new driving certificate in the name of Alexander Duggan to hire a car for the following morning. He also asked the man at the hotel desk to get him a room in a hotel at one of the towns along the coast. The man managed to find him a room in a small hotel in Zeebrugge.

♦

While the Jackal was shopping in Brussels, Viktor Kowalski was telephoning Josef Grzybowski in Marseilles.

JoJo sounded nervous when he spoke. 'It is true,' he told Kowalski. 'Little Sylvie has been getting thinner and weaker, and is now in bed all the time. She is going to die, my friend.'

'Are you at the same flat?' asked Kowalski.

'No, we have moved to a newer, larger one,' said JoJo, and gave him an address.

'How long do the doctors say Sylvie will live?' asked Kowalski.

'A week, perhaps two or three,' said JoJo.

Kowalski put down the telephone. He was confused. There was nobody he could talk to, and this was one problem that he could not solve with violence.

In his flat in Marseilles, the same flat he had always lived in, JoJo put down the phone. He turned to look at the two secret service men in the room. One was pointing a gun at him, the other was pointing one at JoJo's wife.

'Is he coming?' one of the men asked JoJo.

'He didn't say,' said JoJo. 'He just put down the telephone. But he will come, if he can. He will want to see the girl.'

'Good. Then your part is finished.'

'Then get out of here,' said JoJo. 'Leave us alone.'

'We'll go,' said the other man. 'But you two will come with us. To a nice hotel in the mountains.'

'For how long?' asked JoJo.

'For as long as necessary. Pack your bags.'

'What about Sylvie? She will be home from school at four,' said the woman. 'There will be no one to meet her.'

'We will collect her on the way past the school. Plans have been made. Her teacher has been told that her grandmother is dying and the whole family are going to her deathbed. Now, move!'

An hour later the family were in the back seat of a big Citroën, the two secret service men in the front, driving towards a very private hotel in the mountains.

◆

On Saturday the Jackal swam in the sea at Zeebrugge and walked round the little town. On Sunday he packed his bags and drove through the countryside before turning back to Brussels. He asked the man at the hotel desk for an early call the next morning, and for breakfast in bed and a packed lunch. The man promised to organise these things, and the Jackal went to bed.

◆

In Rome, Viktor Kowalski's weekend was not so relaxed. He did his guard duty as usual, but slept very little when he wasn't working. By Monday morning, he had come to a decision. He was going to Marseilles.

He would not be long, he told himself. Perhaps a day or two. He would tell Colonel Rodin afterwards. Rodin would understand, although he would be very angry, Kowalski decided – but he had to go.

◆

The Jackal reached the forest by midday on Monday. He hid the car behind some trees, five or six miles from the main road. For a while he waited in the shadows, smoking a cigarette and listening to the whisper of the wind through the branches of the trees.

At last he got out of the car and fitted the rifle together, piece by piece. He put twenty bullets into one shirt pocket, and the single explosive bullet into the other. When it was ready, he took from the car a melon that he had bought in Brussels on the afternoon of the day before. Taking these things, together with the string shopping bag, paint, brushes and hunting knife, he locked the car and walked off into the forest.

After ten minutes, he found a clear space. He then put the rifle against a tree and walked a hundred and fifty metres away from it. Next he painted a face on the melon. Then he stuck the knife into a tree, put the melon into the string shopping bag, and hung the bag on the knife.

He closed the two cans of paint and threw them and the brushes away into the trees. Then he walked back to the rifle.

After several shots, he was satisfied. Then he took the explosive bullet from his shirt pocket and put it in the rifle. He aimed at the melon – and fired.

The Jackal walked down to the string shopping bag, which hung almost empty against the tree. Most of the melon now lay on the grass below, leaving only one or two bits of fruit stuck to the bag.

He took the bag and threw it into the trees. Then he pulled the hunting knife from the tree and walked back to the car, collecting the rifle on the way.

◆

The following morning the Jackal had his last meeting with Paul Goossens. The metal tubes – which would contain the rifle – were ready. The Englishman examined them carefully.

He aimed at the melon – and fired.

'Perfect,' he said after a minute or two. 'Exactly what I wanted.' He took the tubes, with the parts of the gun inside them, and put them into a leather bag which he had bought in a shop that morning. He then paid the gun-maker the final two hundred pounds. 'Please remember our conversation about keeping silent,' he said.

'I have not forgotten,' replied the Belgian quietly. He was frightened again. Would this soft-spoken killer try to silence him now? But the Englishman seemed to read his thoughts, and smiled.

'You do not need to worry,' he said. 'I'm not going to hurt you. But if you ever speak of my visits to anyone at all, I shall kill you, you can be sure of that.'

A minute later the door closed behind him and the Belgian was able to relax and count his money.

The Jackal went to the main railway station and put the leather bag into the left-luggage office. He put the ticket into his pocket and went back to his hotel. At four o'clock that afternoon, he was on a plane to London.

CHAPTER 4

The Best Detective in France

Viktor Kowalski caught a plane to Marseilles from Rome on Wednesday morning at 11.15. He had not noticed the two men who had followed his taxi to the airport in a small Fiat car. The same two men watched him climb the steps into the plane. Then they went to a telephone to report that Viktor Kowalski was on his way to Marseilles.

The plane arrived at Marseilles Airport and Kowalski took the airport bus to the Air France offices in the centre of the city. He then got a taxi to a street near to the address JoJo had given him, and waited until the taxi was out of sight. He found the street and the building, and looked at the names beside the letterboxes in the hall. 'Grzybowski: Flat 23', he read, and took the stairs to the second floor.

He pushed the bell of flat 23.

Suddenly, the door opened and he was hit over the head. On each side, the doors of flats 22 and 24 were also thrown open and men ran out. It all happened in less than half a second, but Kowalski knew how to fight. Through the blood which was running down over his eyes, he saw that there were two men in front of him and two others on each side. He needed room to move, so he rushed forward into flat 23.

Inside the room he pulled a gun from his pocket and turned and fired back into the doorway. As he did this, a hand came down on to his arm. The bullet hit the knee of one of the other men, who went down with a loud cry. Then the gun was knocked out of Kowalski's hand. A second later, five men threw themselves on to him.

The fight lasted three minutes. Later, a doctor guessed that Kowalski was hit across the head more than twenty times before they finally managed to control him. By that time, his nose was broken, his face was covered in blood, and he could not move.

Twelve hours later, after a fast drive through France, Kowalski was lying on a bed in a prison room just outside Paris. His eyes were still closed but he was alive – just.

'What did you hit him with, a train?' the doctor who examined him asked Colonel Rolland later.

'It took six men to do that,' replied Colonel Rolland.

'Well, they nearly killed him.'

'I need to question him,' said Rolland.

'If you question him now, he'll either die or he'll go crazy.'

'How long?' asked Rolland.

'Impossible to say,' said the doctor. 'He may wake up tomorrow, or not for days. And then he'll not be fit for questioning for at least another two weeks. And he'll be confused. What he tells you may not make any sense.'

Kowalski opened his eyes three days later, on 10th August, and was questioned the same day. He said very little before he died, but his words were recorded. They made no sense to the three secret service men who listened to the recording afterwards, although they played it several times before typing up a twenty-six page report for Colonel Rolland.

Rolland read the pages, trying to understand what Kowalski had been saying. He read it a second time, more slowly, then a third time, drawing a thick black line of ink through the words and sentences that spoke of Sylvie, Algeria, JoJo and Kovacs. All these he understood, and they did not interest him. This left six pages, and he tried to make sense of the words.

Rome. The three leaders were in Rome, Rolland knew that. But why? There was one word Kowalski had said twice when he was asked this question. The word was 'secret'. What secret? It seemed to be connected with a meeting in Vienna. A meeting for what?

The hours passed, and so did many cups of coffee. Rolland wrote down another word: 'Kleist.' A man called Kleist? Kowalski, being Polish, had probably pronounced the word wrongly. Or was it a place? He picked up the telephone and asked someone to search for a person or place called Kleist in Vienna. The answer was back in ten minutes. There were a lot of people called Kleist in Vienna, but there were only two places – a boys' school, and a hotel. Rolland drew a line under the name of the hotel.

He went back to the report. Kowalski had talked about a 'foreigner' several times, and about a 'killer'. And about someone with fair hair. A killer who was a foreigner, with fair hair? The word for 'jackal' had been crossed out because Rolland had first thought it was Kowalski's name for the man who was questioning him. Now he decided it was the name for the fair-haired killer, the man the three OAS men had met at the Hotel Kleist in Vienna before they had gone to Rome.

Now Rolland understood why so many shops and banks had been robbed in France over the last eight weeks. The fair-haired assassin wanted money for the job. And there was only one job in the world for which an assassin would demand that amount of money.

It was time for Rolland to write his own report. Others would have to know what was happening – and quickly.

◆

By late that afternoon, the President had been informed of everything Colonel Rolland had discovered, and Government Minister Roger Frey had called a meeting. Fourteen men attended. They included Minister Frey, Colonel Rolland, Colonel Saint-Clair de Villauban, who worked closely with the President,

33

Maurice Papon, Chief of Police, Maurice Grimaud, head of the national crime force – the Sûreté Nationale. Also there were Max Fernet, director of France's detective force – the Police Judiciare – and the head of its criminal branch, Maurice Bouvier. The other men were chiefs of other crime departments and security organisations.

Frey was speaking to them. 'You have all read Colonel Rolland's report. And I must tell you that the President does not want any more guards when he appears in public, and he will continue to perform his duties in the usual way. In other words, he does not want people to think that he is frightened by this latest danger.' He looked towards Colonel Rolland. 'Have you any information from Vienna yet, Colonel?'

'Yes,' replied Rolland. 'Rodin took a room at the Hotel Kleist on 15th June, calling himself Schulz. The man at the hotel desk recognised Rodin's photograph. He also remembered that Schulz had a man with him – a big, dangerous-looking man – who must have been Kowalski. Schulz was visited by two men in the morning. Perhaps Casson and Montclair – the hotel man wasn't sure. But he said they stayed in their room all day.'

'Were they visited by a fifth man?' asked Papon.

'During the evening another man joined them for half an hour. He went straight up the stairs, but came down again after a few seconds and used the desk phone to call Schulz's room, number 64. He spoke two sentences in French and then went back up the stairs again. He spent half an hour there, then left. The other two who had visited Schulz left separately. Schulz and the big man stayed for the night, then left after breakfast the next morning. The hotel man described the visitor as tall, with dark glasses and fair hair.'

'So, now that Kowalski is dead, there are only four men in the world who know the identity of this Jackal,' said Papon. 'One is the man himself, and the other three are in a hotel in Rome. Is it possible to get one of them back here?'

The Minister shook his head. 'No. All the hotel's doors, stairs, lifts and fire escapes are guarded. It would need a gun battle to get one of them out alive, and the Italian government would not allow that to happen.'

'This Jackal must be found,' said Colonel Saint-Clair, importantly.

'We know that, Colonel,' said the Minister. 'The question is, how?'

'The protection of the President must depend, when all others have failed, on those who work closely with him,' announced Saint-Clair. 'We, I can promise you, Minister, will do our duty!'

Some of the experienced professionals around the table closed their eyes, tiredly, as they listened to this little man who thought he was so important.

Roger Frey looked across the table at the man sitting beside Saint-Clair. It was Maurice Bouvier, of the Police Judiciare, who was sitting quietly, smoking his pipe.

'What do you think, Bouvier?' asked Frey.

The detective took the pipe out of his mouth and managed to blow smoke into Saint-Clair's face before speaking calmly.

'It seems that the secret service cannot find this man, although some of their men are close to OAS members. Perhaps because not even the OAS know who he is. The border police cannot stop him because they do not know who to stop. None of the security forces of France can do anything because they do not have a name. It seems to me that we must first get this man's name. With a name we get a face, with a face there is a passport, and with a passport we can find him. But to find the name, and to do it in secret, is a job for a detective.'

'And who is the best detective in France?' asked the Minister, quietly.

35

Bouvier thought for a few seconds, then said, 'The best detective in France, gentlemen, is Claude Lebel.'

'Bring him here,' said the Minister.

◆

Claude Lebel came out of the meeting after fifty minutes. He was a small, quiet man, with soft brown eyes. He and Bouvier talked together in Bouvier's car as they drove away.

'Do you want a new office for this job?' asked Bouvier.

'No, I prefer my own,' replied Lebel.

'Is there anyone you want to help you?'

'Yes, Caron,' said Lebel. Caron was one of the younger detectives, who had worked with Lebel before.

'OK, you can have Caron. One more thing. Before I left the meeting, Frey suggested that all those who were there tonight are regularly informed of your progress. You will have to meet with them every evening at ten o'clock, and tell them of any developments.'

'Oh, no!'

'Yes, I'm afraid so. We don't know when the Jackal is going to try to assassinate the President. It could be tomorrow morning, or it could be a month from now. Just try to find him as quickly as you can, OK?'

Ten minutes later, Claude Lebel was back in his office. There was a knock on the door. It was Lucien Caron.

'I have been told to report to you,' said Caron.

'Yes,' said Lebel. 'First you can read this.' He gave Caron Colonel Rolland's report, then cleared all the other papers off his desk while the young detective was reading it.

Caron finished reading and looked up. He looked shocked.

'Now I will give you details of my meeting with Minister Frey,' said Lebel. And for thirty minutes, Caron listened in silence.

When Lebel had finished speaking, Caron thought for a

moment, then said, 'They have given you this job because nobody else wants it. And if you fail —'

'Yes, Lucien, I know,' said Lebel. 'There's nothing I can do. I've been given the job, and we just have to do it.'

'Where do we start?' asked Caron.

'I want to speak to the chiefs of police in seven countries: the United States, Britain, Belgium, Holland, Italy, West Germany and South Africa. Organise it by six o'clock tomorrow morning.'

'Yes, Chief,' replied Caron, and reached for the phone.

Outside, the clock of Notre Dame sounded midnight, and the world passed into the morning of 12th August.

♦

Colonel Raoul Saint-Clair de Villauban arrived home just before midnight. He opened the front door of his flat and heard the voice of his most recent girlfriend call him from the bedroom.

'Is that you, Raoul?'

'Yes, my love. Of course it's me. Have you been lonely?'

Jacqueline came running from the bedroom in her nightdress. She threw her arms round his neck and kissed him.

'Why are you so late?' she said. 'I've been waiting.'

'Nothing for you to worry about, my dear,' said Saint-Clair.

She turned away from him. 'You never explain,' she said, sounding annoyed. 'I've been worrying for hours. You've never been as late as this before.'

'I've been very busy, my love. It seems the OAS are still after the President. They've hired a foreign assassin to try to kill him.' Jacqueline listened as Saint-Clair talked . . . and talked . . .

Half an hour after that, Saint-Clair was asleep. Beside him, Jacqueline lay looking up at the ceiling. She was shocked by what she had learned. She waited until the clock beside her said two o'clock. Then she quietly got out of bed, left the bedroom, and walked to the telephone in the living room.

37

'*Why are you so late?*'

She waited until a sleepy voice answered, then spoke quickly for two minutes before putting the phone down again. A minute later she was back in bed, trying to sleep.

♦

Later, a middle-aged teacher used a telephone at an all-night post office near the railway station to talk to a man in Rome. 'Listen,' he said. 'I don't have much time. Write this down: 'Valmy to Poitiers. They know about the Jackal. Repeat. They know about the Jackal. Kowalski was taken. Talked before dying. Message ends.' Have you got that?'

'Yes,' said the man in Rome. 'I'll pass it on.'

Valmy put down the phone and paid the woman behind the desk. Then he hurried out.

♦

In Rome, at 7.55, an angry Marc Rodin got the message that Kowalski had talked. He immediately tried to remember just what the guard knew. The meeting in Vienna, of course, and the name of the hotel; and the three men who had been at the meeting. But this would not be news to the secret service. But what did Kowalski know about the Jackal? How had he known the name 'Jackal'? Then Rodin remembered saying 'Good night, Mr Jackal' outside the door of the hotel room when Kowalski had been near them.

Rodin was angry with himself. He realised that Kowalski did not know the killer's real name – only he, Montclair and Casson knew that. But the secret service would guess what Kowalski had guessed – that the fair-haired man was a killer. Now the security plans for de Gaulle would tighten. There would be no chance for an assassin to get him. He would have to stop the Jackal, and ask for the money back.

He called the guard outside the hotel room, and sent him to

the post office to collect the mail and to telephone a London number.

◆

The Jackal got up early that morning. He made himself a quick breakfast of eggs, orange juice and black coffee, then dressed. An hour later he took his luggage down to the corner of the street and stopped a taxi.

'Heathrow Airport,' he told the driver.

As the taxi moved away, the telephone in his flat began to ring.

◆

It was ten o'clock when the guard returned to the hotel. He told Rodin that he had tried for thirty minutes to get a reply from the London number, but had not been successful.

'What's the matter?' asked Casson after the guard had gone. He and Montclair were with Rodin.

Rodin explained.

'You've got to stop him!' said Montclair. 'They'll search until they find him now.'

'They're looking for a tall, fair-haired foreigner,' said Rodin. 'In August there are a million foreigners in France. As far as we know the police have no name, no face, no passport. And if the Jackal telephones Valmy, he will hear the news and be able to get out again. But it depends how confident he feels. Remember, he's a professional. I can't stop him now. Nobody can stop the Jackal now. It's too late.'

◆

The Jackal arrived at Brussels Airport just after midday and left his three main pieces of luggage in a locker there. He took a bag with him into town. It contained the things he would need immediately, including some pieces of cloth and some plaster. At the main railway station he went to the left-luggage office. There he collected the bag containing the gun, which he had left there a week earlier.

He found a small hotel near the station and got a room. Then, with the door safely locked behind him, he put the plaster and pieces of cloth on the bed and started work.

It took more than two hours for the plaster to dry. During this time he sat with his heavy foot and leg resting on a chair, smoked cigarettes, and looked out of the window at the rooftops. The bag that had contained the gun was now empty.

Before he finally left the room, the Jackal pushed the bag under the bed and went downstairs, carrying his other bag. The man behind the desk was eating his lunch in a room at the back, and the Jackal was able to get out of the hotel without being noticed.

It was difficult to walk with his leg in plaster, but he found a taxi and was soon on his way back to the airport. At the ticket office, he gave the girl his passport, and she smiled at him.

'I believe you have a ticket for Milan, in the name of Duggan,' he said.

She looked at the names for the afternoon flight to Milan. 'Yes,' she said. 'Mr Duggan. You need to pay for the ticket.'

The Jackal paid in cash.

Everybody on the plane was kind and helpful when they saw his leg in plaster. The Jackal smiled bravely at them.

They arrived at Milan soon after six o'clock that evening and the Jackal took a taxi to the railway station and went to the left-luggage office. Here he left three bags, but kept one containing the long French army coat. Then he went down to the men's toilet, where he could cut the plaster off his leg in private. He took the metal tubes containing the gun from the plaster and put them into the bag with the coat. He then pushed the pieces of cloth and the plaster down the toilet, and quickly went up into the main hall of the station again.

Next the Jackal asked a railway worker to get his other bags from the left–luggage office, and then went to change his English money into Italian money. Two minutes later he was travelling towards the Hotel Continentale, where he had a room in the name of Duggan.

The next day, 13th August, would be a very busy day.

CHAPTER 5

A Man Called Calthrop

Two men were meeting in a quiet bar near the River Thames in London. One of them was Police Superintendent Bryn Thomas; the other was Barrie Lloyd, a British secret service man. They were old friends, and after searching unsuccessfully through his own files, Thomas wanted the secret service man's help.

He explained about the urgent telephone request his boss had received from a detective called Lebel in Paris early that morning. The other man was silent for a moment, then he said, 'An assassin, and the French are worried? Then the killer is after de Gaulle.'

'I agree,' said Thomas. 'But the French aren't saying anything.'

Lloyd drank his beer and thought for a few minutes. 'Nineteen sixty-one,' he said at last. 'The Dominican Republic. A man called Trujillo, head of the government there, was assassinated on a lonely road. Our man there came back to London and we shared an office for a while. He said that some people thought Trujillo's speeding car was stopped by a single rifle shot from a hundred and fifty metres away, by someone who was extremely good with a gun. The bullet went through a little window on the driver's side – the only window that wasn't protected from bullets – and hit the driver through the neck. Then Trujillo's enemies were able to bomb the car. The strange thing was, some people said the gunman was an Englishman.'

'This man . . . did he have a name?'

'I don't remember. I'll have to check the files,' said Lloyd. 'I'll telephone you if there's anything that might help.'

The two men got up from their table and walked to the door.

'Thanks, Barrie,' said Thomas. 'There's probably no connection, but we should check.'

◆

While Thomas and Lloyd were talking above the waters of the Thames, Claude Lebel was attending a progress meeting with the Minister and the other men who had been at the first meeting.

The Minister was telling them that every Customs officer on every border in France had received orders to check through the luggage of tall, fair-haired male foreigners entering France, and to look carefully for any passports that might be forged.

One of the other department chiefs had news to report. 'A telephone call was made from a post office near the Gare du Nord railway station to the Rome hotel where the OAS chiefs are staying. Since their appearance there eight weeks ago, all calls to that number have been reported to us. But this call was put through before the girl at the telephone company realised that it was one of the numbers on her list. She listened to the message, which was: "Valmy to Poitiers. They know about the Jackal. Repeat. They know about the Jackal. Kowalski was taken. Talked before dying. Message ends." Then she telephoned us.'

'Did you get Valmy at the post office?' asked Lebel.

'No, we missed him by a few minutes because the telephone girl didn't call us immediately.'

There was silence in the room for several seconds.

'How did they find out?' asked Lebel quietly.

'Marseilles,' said Colonel Rolland, after a moment. 'We used an old friend of Kowalski's – JoJo Grzybowski – to bring him from Rome. The man has a wife and daughter. We kept them until Kowalski was with us, then we let them return home. All I wanted from Kowalski was information about his employers. We knew nothing about the Jackal at that time. There was no reason why they should not know we had got Kowalski – then. Later, of

'These are stupid mistakes!'

course, things changed. I expect JoJo told Valmy. Sorry.'

'These are stupid mistakes!' said Colonel Saint-Clair angrily.

'Perhaps the Colonel would like to take responsibility for finding the Jackal,' said Rolland.

Saint-Clair began to examine his papers closely, but said nothing.

'Perhaps,' said the Minister, 'it's a good thing they've discovered that we know about their hired killer. Won't they stop the assassination now?'

'Of course,' said Saint-Clair, 'the Minister is right. They would be crazy to continue now.'

'Would they?' said Lebel, quietly. 'We still don't know the man's name. Perhaps he will just be more careful now – use false papers, change his appearance . . .'

They were all quiet for a moment, then Minister Frey said to Lebel, 'Give us your report. You are the detective – we are here to help if we can.'

Lebel described what he had done since the evening before, then continued, 'I believe, gentlemen, that our man can only be on the files of a foreign police force, if he is on any file at all. I spoke to the police chiefs of seven countries this morning and replies have come in during today. Here they are.' He began to read. 'Holland, nothing. Italy, several killers they know about but none who would do a political killing. Britain, nothing yet, but they are still checking.'

'Slow, as usual,' said Saint-Clair.

'But very careful, our English friends,' said Lebel. He went on reading. 'America. Perhaps two. A man called Charles – 'Chuck' – Arnold. The police are trying to find out where he is at the moment. And Marco Vitellino, who lives in Venezuela.'

There was complete silence in the room as Lebel went on.

'Belgium. One. Jules Berenger. Believed to be living in Central America. The Belgian police are still checking where he is at the moment. Germany. One suggestion. Hans–Dieter Kassel, who they think lives in Madrid. Lastly, South Africa. One. Piet Schuyper. They think he lives in West Africa somewhere.' Lebel looked round at the others. 'I only tried seven countries, but I expect to have all the files of these men by midday tomorrow. That is all.'

The Minister picked up the papers in front of him. 'Thank you. We will meet again tomorrow, gentlemen.'

Lebel was pleased to get outside and to breathe the soft night air of Paris. The clocks in the city sounded midnight and then it was Tuesday, 13th August.

◆

It was just after midnight when Barrie Lloyd telephoned his friend Superintendent Thomas at his home in London.

'I found a copy of the report we were talking about,' said Lloyd.

'Was there a name?' asked Thomas.

'Yes, a British businessman on the island, who disappeared about that time. His name was Charles Calthrop.'

'Thanks, Barrie.' Thomas put down the telephone.

◆

The Jackal got up at 7.30 that Tuesday morning, took one thousand pounds from a secret hiding place in his bag, and by nine o'clock was walking down the Via Manzoni looking for banks. For two hours he went from one to another, changing the English pounds. Two hundred were changed into Italian money, the other eight hundred into French money.

After that he began looking for a garage which he could rent. He found one in a small street near Garibaldi Station, and hired it for two days.

That afternoon he hired a 1962 Alfa Romeo two-seater car for two weeks, explaining that he was on holiday and wanted to drive around Italy. He drove the Alfa Romeo back to the Hotel Continentale car park, went up to his room and collected the pieces of the rifle, then drove to the lock-up garage near Garibaldi Station.

He worked under the car for two hours. When he had finished, the tubes were almost impossible to see in their hiding place under the Alfa, and they would soon be covered with dust and dirt.

It was getting dark when the Jackal drove back to the hotel. After a bath and a change of clothes, he went down to the hotel desk, paid his bill and asked for a wake-up call at 5.30 the following morning.

◆

Superintendent Thomas had a man waiting outside the Passport Office when it opened at nine o'clock in the morning. After some time, the man got copies of six passport forms in the name of Charles Calthrop and hurried back with them to Thomas.

One form was dated after January 1961, the month and year Trujillo was assassinated in the Dominican Republic. Of the other five, one man seemed too old. He was sixty-five by August 1963. Two of the other four had an address in London.

Police outside London found one Charles Calthrop in the accounts department of the factory where he worked. He went home with them and showed them his passport. There was no Dominican Republic passport stamp in it.

The other man outside London was away from home at a hotel in Blackpool, but he allowed the police to borrow a house key from his neighbour, enter his house, and look at his passport. There was no Dominican Republic stamp.

Of the two Charles Calthrops in London, one lived in the flat above his fruit and vegetable shop, and was able to find his passport quickly. Like the others, he had never been to the Dominican Republic.

The fourth and last Calthrop was more difficult to find. The address on his passport form was a flat in north London, but he had left there in December 1960. Thomas soon discovered, though, that Charles Harold Calthrop had an unlisted telephone number at an address in west London. The flat was visited by two of Thomas's men, but the door was locked and there was no reply to the repeated rings on the bell. Nobody in the other flats seemed to know where Mr Calthrop was.

Thomas then spoke to the Tax Office, and by six o'clock that evening he knew that Charles Harold Calthrop had been unemployed for the past year, and had been abroad before that. During the years 1960–61, he had been employed by a company that sold guns.

By eight o'clock that evening, Thomas was on his way to see the head of the company, Mr Patrick Monson. From him, Thomas learnt that Calthrop had worked for Monson's company for less than a year. More importantly, during December 1960 and January 1961 he had been sent to Cuidad Trujillo to try to sell guns to Trujillo's police chief.

'Why did Calthrop leave the Dominican Republic in such a hurry?' Thomas wanted to know.

'Because Trujillo was killed, of course,' replied Monson. 'How could Calthrop sell guns to Trujillo's enemies – a future new government there – when he had been trying to sell them to Trujillo only a few days before? Of course he had to get out.'

It made sense, Thomas had to agree. 'Why did he leave the company?' he asked Monson.

The other man thought for a moment. 'Let's just say that we were not completely satisfied that Calthrop was loyal to the company. We believe he shared our company secrets with others.'

On the journey back to London, Thomas thought about what

Monson had told him. One thing worried him. Monson had said that Calthrop didn't know much about rifles when he joined the company. If that was true, why was he hired to stop Trujillo's car on a fast road with a single shot? Or was Calthrop in fact not a killer at all?

There was more news waiting for him back at the office. The policeman who had visited Calthrop's address had found a neighbour who had been out at work all day. The woman said Mr Calthrop had left some days before and had said he was going to Scotland for a driving holiday. In the back of the car, parked in the street below outside, the woman had seen what looked like some fishing equipment.

Superintendent Thomas suddenly felt cold, although the office was warm. As the detective finished talking, one of his colleagues came in.

'I've just thought of something, sir,' he said.

'Go on.'

'Do you speak French?'

'No,' said Thomas, 'do you?'

'Yes, my mother was French. This assassin the French are looking for, he's calling himself the Jackal, right?'

'Yes.'

'Well, "jackal" in French is "chacal". C–H–A–C–A–L. He must be stupid to choose a name that's made up of the first three letters of his first name, and the first three letters of his –'

'What!' shouted Thomas. And he picked up the telephone.

CHAPTER 6

The British Connection

At the third progress meeting Lebel was reading from the latest reports from the police in some of the other countries. 'Kassel. Now living quietly in Madrid. He has never worked for the OAS. Chuck Arnold. He's selling guns in Colombia, but he is being watched by the American secret service. Vitellino. They are still looking for him, but he is short and fat with black hair, so I think we can forget him. Piet Schuyper is now head of the private army of a company in West Africa. He is working there now. Jules Berenger was killed in Guatemala three months ago.' He looked up at the fourteen pairs of cold, questioning eyes that were watching him.

'That's all?' asked Colonel Rolland.

'That's all,' said Lebel.

'Is that all that the "best detective in France" has produced?' said Saint-Clair. He looked angrily at Bouvier and Lebel.

'It seems, gentlemen,' the Minister said to the two detectives, 'that we are back where we started.'

'Yes, I'm afraid we are,' said Lebel.

There was a knock on the door. 'Come in,' said the Minister.

The door opened and one of the Minister's men said that there was an urgent telephone call for Lebel.

Lebel went to take the call and returned in five minutes. When he came back, Saint-Clair was still complaining about the poor progress the detectives were making. He stopped speaking when Lebel sat down again.

'I think, gentlemen, we have the name of the man we are looking for,' said Lebel.

Thirty minutes later the meeting ended and everyone was feeling better. They had agreed that it would now be possible to search France for a man called Charles Calthrop, to find him and, if necessary, to kill him. And if he had not yet arrived in France, they would catch him when he did.

♦

'We will soon have the man they call Calthrop,' Colonel Raoul Saint-Clair de Villauban told Jacqueline that night as they lay in bed together.

After they had made love and he finally went to sleep, the bedroom clock sounded midnight, and it was 14th August.

And in the early hours of that morning, two detectives in London searched Charles Calthrop's flat. By six o'clock they were driving back to Superintendent Thomas's office with a bag full of Calthrop's papers, including his passport.

'Look!' one of the detectives said to Thomas, pointing excitedly at one of the pages of the passport. 'He was in the Dominican Republic in December 1960! This is our man!'

Thomas took the passport, looked at it for a moment, then looked out of the window. 'Yes, this is our man. But think for a moment. We are holding his passport in our hands . . . so . . . if he's not travelling with this passport, then what is he travelling with? Give me the phone and get me Paris.'

♦

By that same time, the Jackal had been driving for fifty minutes and the city of Milan was far behind him. The roof of the Alfa was down and the sun was warm on his head. At 8.50 he arrived at the French border. He had waited in a line of traffic for thirty minutes before a policeman took his passport and looked at it carefully.

'One moment, sir,' he said, and went away.

He came back a few minutes later with another man, who was not wearing a uniform.

'Good morning, sir,' said the other man.

'Good morning,' said the Jackal.

'This is your passport?'

'Yes.'

'Why are you visiting France?'

'I'm on holiday,' said the Jackal.

'Is the car yours?'

'No. It is a hired car. I had business in Italy, but then had a week with nothing to do before returning to Milan. So I hired a car to take a little holiday.'

'You have papers for the car?'

The Jackal gave the man the international driving certificate and the car-hire papers.

'You have luggage, sir? Please bring it into the Customs hall.' The man walked away, and the policeman helped the Jackal carry the bags into the hall.

Before leaving Milan the Jackal had taken the old army coat, trousers and shoes of André Martin, the Frenchman who did not exist, and pushed them into the back of the car. The medals were in his pocket.

Two Customs officers examined each bag. Through the window, the Jackal saw another man examining the engine of the Alfa. The man then looked at the old clothes but pushed them back again. Fortunately he did not look under the car.

Ten minutes later the Jackal had his passport back and was driving into Menton. After a relaxed breakfast in a café, he drove on towards Monaco, Nice and Cannes.

♦

At nine o'clock, in his London office, Superintendent Thomas spoke to eight detectives.

'Is the car yours?'

'All right, we're looking for a man. There's no need for me to tell you why we want him, it's not important for you to know. What is important is that we get him, and get him fast. We think he's abroad at this moment, travelling with a false passport.' He gave each of them a photograph of Calthrop, taken from the picture in the man's passport. 'This is what he looks like, but he probably won't look like that now. I want you to go to the Passport Office and get a list of every passport form received in the last fifty days. If that produces nothing, go back another fifty days. It's going to be hard work.'

He described the usual way of getting a false passport, which was in fact the method used by the Jackal.

'When you get the list from the Passport Office, check birth certificates and death certificates at the Office of Births, Marriages and Deaths. Try to find one passport form for a man who isn't alive any more. The person using that name will probably be the man we want. Get started.'

◆

Just after eleven o'clock that morning, the Jackal arrived in Cannes and went to the Majestic Hotel. From the telephone box in the hall, he rang a Paris number: MOLITOR 5901.

'Hello, this is the Jackal,' he said a minute or two later.

'This is Valmy,' said the man at the other end. 'We've been trying to find you for two days!'

The Jackal listened in silence for the next ten minutes, except to ask one or two short questions. Then he left the telephone box.

He sat at one of the tables outside the hotel, and looked out at the sea while he drank a cup of coffee and smoked a cigarette. He was being hunted. Valmy had told him to stop everything and go home. He had agreed, though, that this was not an order from Rodin. The Jackal thought hard. Valmy had spoken of a detective called Lebel. What did Lebel know? That they were hunting for a tall, fair-haired foreigner. There must be thousands of men like that in France in August. And they were looking for a man carrying the passport of Charles Calthrop. Well, he was Alexander Duggan, and could prove it.

From now on, with Kowalski dead, nobody, not even Rodin and his friends, knew who he was or where he was. He was on his own, and that was the way he had always wanted to be.

But it would be more dangerous now. So . . . go back, or go on? That was the question he had to answer.

He asked for his bill for the coffee. It was expensive. To live this kind of life a man needed to be rich. He looked at the blue sea, the beautiful girls walking along the beach, the expensive cars driving past. This was what he wanted. He was used to good clothes, expensive meals, a comfortable flat, a good car, beautiful women. To go back meant the end of all that.

The Jackal paid the bill, climbed into the Alfa and drove away from the Majestic Hotel – and towards the centre of France.

By that evening, he was entering the little town of Gap. He took a room at the Hotel du Cerf, had a bath and changed his clothes, then went down for dinner.

The food was excellent. The Jackal was finishing his meal when he heard a woman at another table tell the waiter, 'I'll take my coffee in the room next door. The chairs are more comfortable and there are magazines to read.' She was a beautiful woman – in her late thirties, the Jackal guessed. A few minutes later, he told the waiter that he too would take his coffee in the room next door.

◆

Superintendent Thomas received the telephone call from the Office of Births, Marriages and Deaths at 10.15 that evening.

'Alexander James Duggan,' the man on the telephone said.

'What about him?' said Thomas.

'Born 3rd April 1929. Requested a passport on 14th July this year. The passport was sent to the address on the form on 17th July. It will probably be a place where mail can be sent and left until it is picked up.'

'Why?' said Thomas.

'Because Alexander James Duggan was killed in a road accident on 8th November 1931, when he was two-and-a-half years old.'

Thomas thought for a moment. 'How many more passport forms do you have to check?' he asked.

'About three hundred,' said the other detective.

'Leave the other men to finish checking,' said Thomas. 'Go and check that address where the passport was sent. Telephone me as soon as you have found it, then bring me back all the details about the false Duggan, and the photograph that was sent in with the passport form. I want to have a look at this man Calthrop with his new face.'

It was just before eleven o'clock when Thomas learned that the address was a small shop in Paddington. The owner, who lived above the shop, often took in mail for customers – for a price. He could not remember a regular customer called Duggan, and he did not recognise the photograph of Calthrop.

'Bring him in,' Thomas told his man, 'and come back here yourself.'

Then he picked up the telephone and asked for Paris.

◆

A second time, the telephone call came through during the evening progress meeting. Lebel had explained that he was sure Calthrop was not in France using his own name, but that he might already be in the country using a false passport.

'You mean he might be here, in France, even in the centre of Paris?' said Saint-Clair, shocked.

'Yes, but the killer cannot know what progress we have made,' said Lebel. 'And we have a good chance of finding him as soon as we know his new name.'

It was then that the telephone call came through for Lebel. This time he was gone for twenty minutes. When he came back, the others listened in silence as he gave them the details of the call.

'What do we do now?' asked the Minister when Lebel had finished.

'We search quietly for Duggan with his new face, while the British police check airport ticket offices, boats and trains,' said Lebel. 'If they find him first, they will take him if he is in Britain, or inform us if he has left there. If we find him inside France, we take him. If we find him in another country, we can either wait for him to enter and get him at the border, or . . . you can act in some other way. But until I find him, gentlemen, I would be grateful if you would agree to do things my way.'

Nobody said anything, but they knew they had no choice in the matter. This little man was in control. Even Saint-Clair de Villauban was silent.

It was not until he was at home soon after midnight that he found someone to listen to his angry complaints about the detective. Saint-Clair had been sure that the Jackal would not continue when he learnt what the government knew. He had been wrong – and he didn't like being wrong. Especially when some unimportant little detective was proved right.

His lover listened as he talked. Later, when he was asleep, she got out of bed and went to make a short phone call.

CHAPTER 7

Colette

Madame Colette de la Chalonnière paused outside her room and turned towards the young Englishman who had walked with her to her door. It had been a pleasant evening and she still had not decided if she wanted it to end there.

She was a married woman staying for a single night in a small hotel. Although she had had lovers before, she was not in the habit of allowing complete strangers into her bed. But she was feeling particularly sensitive about herself that night.

She looked five years younger, and sometimes felt ten years younger, than her age, but her son was a young man now and did not live at home. And her husband was too busy chasing young girls in Paris to come down to their country house for the summer. She knew that, although she was still beautiful, she was alone.

She had been thinking of these things while drinking her coffee after dinner. 'It would be nice,' she had thought, 'if someone would tell me that I am beautiful, and that they wanted me.' And at that moment the Englishman had come up and said, 'May I take my coffee with you?' and had sat down next to her.

She guessed he was about thirty-five, the best age for a man. Although he was English, he spoke French easily; he was quite good-looking, and could be amusing. She had enjoyed his attention and their conversation, and it was nearly midnight when she got up from her chair and explained that she had to leave early the following morning.

He had walked up the stairs with her, and they had stopped for a few moments at a window to look out at the sleeping

'May I take my coffee with you?'

countryside, until she noticed that he was not looking at the view but at her.

Now she had her hand on the handle of the door. Perhaps it was the wine, or the scene in the moonlight, but she was hoping that he might kiss her. Then, suddenly, his lips were on hers, and she felt his strong arms around her.

When she felt the door behind her open, she moved out of his arms and back into the room. He stepped in and closed the door after him.

◆

Now that they had the name Duggan, French Customs were able to pass information to Lebel during the night. They were able to tell him that Alexander Duggan entered France on a train from Brussels on 22nd July, and caught another train from Paris to Brussels on 31st July.

Then a hotel card came from the police. It was in the name of Duggan, and showed that he had stayed in a small hotel near the Place de la Madeleine between 22nd July and 30th July.

'Why does the Jackal stay in hotels?' thought Lebel. 'Why doesn't he stay with friends of the OAS? Perhaps because he cannot be sure that they will keep their mouths shut. So he works alone.'

◆

'I have to get up in two hours,' Colette told the Jackal. 'You must go back to your room, lover.'

He dressed, then sat on the edge of the bed and looked down at her as she lay there.

'It was good?' he asked.

'Very good,' she said. 'And you?'

He smiled. 'What do you think?'

She laughed. 'What is your name?' she asked.

He thought for a moment. 'Alex,' he lied.

61

'Well, Alex, it was very good. But it is also time you went back to your own room.'

He kissed her on the lips. 'Then good night, Colette,' he said. A second later he was gone, and the door closed behind him. It was 5.15.

♦

At seven in the morning, the local policeman cycled up to the Hotel du Cerf. The manager was already busy behind the hotel desk when the policeman entered.

'Here you are,' said the manager, 'bright and early.'

'As usual,' said the policeman. 'It's a long ride out here on a bicycle, and I always leave you until the last.'

The manager smiled. 'Because we make the best coffee,' he said. 'Marie-Louise, bring our friend here a cup of coffee.'

The country policeman smiled with pleasure.

'Here are our cards,' said the hotel manager, and gave the policeman the little white cards filled in the evening before by the new guests. 'There were only three new ones last night.'

The policeman put the cards into his pocket, and waited for his coffee. When it arrived, he talked and joked with Marie-Louise for a while, then cycled back to the police station at Gap. It was eight o'clock when he arrived with the cards. Later that day, they would travel to Lyons, and even later to Paris.

♦

At ten o'clock on Thursday morning, the telephone beside Superintendent Thomas rang and he picked it up.

'Hello,' he said.

One of Thomas's detectives answered. 'Duggan left London on a flight on Monday morning. No doubt about the name. Alexander Duggan. Paid cash at the airport for the ticket.'

'Where to?' said Thomas. 'Paris?'

'No, Brussels.'

Thomas thought quickly. 'Keep checking. If he came back from Brussels, I want to know.'

'Right. What about the search in Britain for the real Calthrop? It's keeping a lot of police all over the country busy, and they're complaining.'

Thomas thought for a moment. 'Tell them to stop looking,' he said. 'I'm almost certain he's gone.' He picked up another phone and asked for Lebel's office in Paris.

Lebel took the call, then he telephoned the police in Brussels.

♦

The Jackal got up when the sun was already high over the hills, promising another beautiful summer day. Soon after 10.30 he drove the Alfa into town and went into the post office to telephone Paris. When he came out again twenty minutes later, he was looking serious and was in a hurry. He went to a shop and bought a large can of dark blue paint, a smaller can of white, and two brushes. Then he returned to the Hotel du Cerf and asked for his bill.

While it was being prepared, he went upstairs to pack, then came down to pay the man behind the desk. Later, the man would say that the Englishman seemed nervous. What he did not say, because he had not seen it, was that while he was in the back room for a moment or two, the Englishman had looked at his list of guests. He had found the name: Madame Colette de la Chalonnière, and her address in Corrèze.

A few moments after the Englishman had paid his bill, the Alfa was speeding away from the hotel.

♦

More messages arrived for Claude Lebel at midday. The police in Brussels telephoned to say that Duggan had spent only five hours in the city on Monday, then left on the afternoon flight to Milan. Next, Lebel received a call saying that Alexander Duggan had crossed the border from Italy into France the morning before.

Lebel was very angry. 'Nearly thirty hours ago!' he shouted. Then he spoke to Caron. 'Telephone Superintendent Thomas in London and tell him that the Jackal is inside France, and that we will look for him now. Thank him for his help.'

As Caron finished the London call, the police at Lyons came on the telephone. Lebel listened for several minutes, then smiled at Caron. He covered the telephone with his hand for a moment.

'We've got him!' he said to Caron. 'He's staying at the Hotel du Cerf in Gap for two days, starting last night.' He uncovered the telephone again and spoke to the man at the other end. 'Now listen, I can't explain why we want this man Duggan, but this is what I want you to do . . .'

He spoke for ten minutes and, as he finished, the telephone on Caron's desk rang. Caron listened for a minute, put down the telephone, then said to Lebel, 'Duggan entered France in a white Alfa Romeo, number MI–61741.'

Lebel thought for a moment. 'He'll kill anyone who tries to stop him. The gun must be in the car somewhere. The important thing is he's staying at the hotel for two nights. We must get him there. Come on, let's go.'

While he was speaking, the police at Gap were placing guards at all roads leaving the town. Their orders came from Lyons. Just outside Paris, a plane was ready to fly Lebel and Caron to Gap.

♦

Even under the shadows of the trees in the forest, it was a very hot afternoon. With his shirt off, the Jackal worked on the car for two hours. Earlier, he had turned the Alfa off the main road and had taken a road into the hills. Soon after that, he had found a path leading to the forest.

By the middle of the afternoon, he had finished painting, and stood back to look at the car. The Alfa was now a dark blue, and most of the paint was already dry. Next he painted new imaginary numbers on the back of the car's number plates – the last two were 75, the numbers for the city of Paris, and the commonest type of car number in France.

The Jackal fixed the number plates back on to the car, then threw away the rest of the paint and the two brushes. He put his shirt back on and drove back to the main road. High above him, he watched a small plane on its way east.

It was 3.41.

In the main street in the village of Die, a motorcycle policeman waved at him, telling him to stop and move across to the right-hand side of the road, and moments later ten police cars went past him, down the road from which the Jackal had just come. He could see the policemen sitting in the backs of the vehicles, with guns across their knees.

When they had gone past, the motorcycle policeman turned back to the Jackal and waved at him to continue, and the blue Alfa disappeared round the corner, going west.

♦

Lebel and Caron arrived at the Hotel du Cerf at 4.50. The small plane that had brought them had landed on the other side of the town, and they had been driven to the hotel in a police car.

Caron questioned the hotel manager. Five minutes later, the building was full of policemen. They questioned the people working at the hotel, examined the bedroom where the Jackal had slept, and searched the gardens. Lebel walked outside and looked up at the hills around the hotel.

Caron joined him. 'You really think he's gone, Chief?' he said. 'He was expected to stay for two days.'

'Yes, he's gone,' said Lebel. 'He decided to leave sometime this morning, and he left. The question is: where has he gone? And does he know that we know who he is?'

'But how could he?' said Caron.

'I don't know,' said Lebel. 'Use the police radio in one of the cars and send out a message for all police and Customs officers to look for a white Alfa Romeo, Italian, number MI−61741. I'll speak to the chief of police at Lyons, then let's get back to Paris.'

♦

It was two o'clock in the morning of Friday 16th August when the Jackal passed a sign saying 'Egletons, 6 kilometres' and decided to leave the car in one of the forests near the road.

He found a path leading into the trees and drove through the dark shadows for almost a kilometre before stopping. He turned off the lights and got out of the Alfa.

He spent an hour under the car, and at last the tubes containing the rifle were free from their hiding place. He packed them in the bag with the old clothes and army coat. He then covered the car in tree branches until it was hidden.

The Jackal then picked up the other two bags, and carried all three back to the road. It took him an hour to get there, and he sat down at the side of the road to wait for a bus.

At 5.50, a car stopped and the driver shouted to him.

'Has your car broken down?' He was a farmer.

'No,' said the Jackal. 'I've got a weekend away from camp, so I'm getting rides home. A car brought me to Ussel last night, and I decided to walk on towards Tulle. I've got an uncle there who can get me a ride to Bordeaux. This was as far as I got.' He smiled at the driver.

The farmer laughed. 'Crazy, walking through the night up here. Jump in. I'll take you into Egletons – you can try to get a ride from there.'

They got to the little town at 6.45. The Jackal thanked the

'The question is: where has he gone?'

farmer, then walked round the back of the station and found a café. He went inside.

'Is there a taxi in the town?' he asked the barman as he drank his coffee. The barman gave him a number, and the Jackal telephoned the taxi company. There would be a car in half an hour, he was told.

It arrived at 7.30, an old Renault.

'Do you know the village of Haute Chalonnière?' he asked the driver.

'Of course,' said the driver.

'How far?'

'Eighteen kilometres.' The man pointed towards the mountains. 'In the hills.'

The Jackal put his luggage into the car.

He asked the driver to leave him in front of the café in the centre of the village. There was no need for the taxi-driver to know that he was going to Colette's house.

He took his luggage into the café and sat at a table. He asked for a glass of wine. When the woman brought it, he said: 'How far is the house of Madame de la Chalonnière?'

'Two kilometres,' said the woman.

'I have to get there,' said the Jackal.

The farm workers at the other tables watched him but said nothing. The Jackal took a large French bank note from his pocket.

'How much is the wine, Madame?' he asked.

She looked at the note, and the Jackal heard the men behind him whispering.

'There is a man in the village who might drive you up there,' said a voice.

The Jackal looked as if he was thinking about it. 'What will you drink, while I'm thinking?' he said.

The farm worker looked at the woman, and she poured another large glass of red wine.

'And your friends?' said the Jackal. 'It's thirsty weather.'

The faces round the other table smiled as the woman poured more glasses of wine.

'Benoit, go and get your car,' said the farm worker, and one of the men drank his wine quickly and went outside.

The advantage of village people, the Jackal thought as he rode in Benoit's car a little later, was that they didn't like talking to strangers – and would keep their mouths shut.

◆

Colette de la Chalonnière sat up in bed and read the letter from her friend again. Then she looked at the photograph of her husband which had been cut from a Paris magazine and which had come with the letter. There he was, looking over the shoulder of a beautiful young film actress who had said that she hoped one day to marry him!

Colette threw the letter and the photograph on to the floor, and got out of bed. She went to look at herself in the long mirror on the wall.

'I am still beautiful,' she told herself. And she remembered the night with the young Englishman, just twenty-four hours before. Why hadn't she stayed on at Gap? Why had she come home to this big empty house? Empty except for Louison, the old gardener, and his wife, Ernestine, who cleaned the rooms and cooked the meals.

There was the sound of an old car stopping outside, and Colette went to the window and looked down. She saw the car drive away again, leaving behind a man with his luggage. She recognised the fair hair, and smiled with pleasure. 'You animal. You beautiful animal,' she thought. 'You followed me.'

◆

Three days later, on the morning of 20th August, a man walking in the forest discovered the blue Alfa Romeo. It was nearly midday when the village policemen reported it to the police at Ussel, and not until five o'clock that afternoon when somebody realised the blue paint was new and that the number plates had been changed.

Claude Lebel got the news just before six o'clock, and immediately gave orders for villages in the area to be searched for Duggan.

Lebel gave the news to the men at the meeting that evening. He also went on to say, 'We know that he bought paint to change the colour of the car, probably in Gap. If he did, then somebody told him that we knew about the white Alfa, and that he was using the name Duggan. He telephoned somebody, or somebody telephoned him with the information. So he got out, fast.'

There was silence.

'Are you seriously suggesting,' somebody said at last, 'that he's getting the information from one of us?'

'I cannot be sure about that,' said Lebel. 'But there is another thing. When the Jackal learnt that we knew about the name Duggan, he did not try to leave France. In other words, he has not changed his plan to assassinate the President.'

◆

Later, Saint-Clair told Jacqueline what Lebel had said. Then went on, 'And he suggested that it was our fault information was getting through to the Jackal! Us! The most important men in France!'

Jacqueline allowed her clothes to fall around her feet, then she put her arms around her lover and whispered, 'Tell me all about it.'

CHAPTER 8

Another Killing

The morning of 21st August was bright and clear. Looking out of the windows of Colette's house, across the hills, everything appeared calm and peaceful, with no sign of the busy police activity in the town of Egletons, eighteen kilometres away.

The Jackal stood at the window of a downstairs room and made his usual telephone call to Paris. He had left Colette asleep in the bedroom upstairs.

'Valmy,' said the voice at the other end. 'Things have started to happen again. They have found the car . . .'

The Jackal listened for two minutes, interrupting only to ask a question. With a final 'Thank you', he put down the telephone and lit a cigarette. What he had just heard, he realised, meant that he must change his plans. He had wanted to stay at Colette's house for another two days, but now he had to leave, and the sooner the better.

There was something else about the telephone call that worried him, though. There had been a slight sound on the line after he had picked up the telephone. It had not happened before during the three days he had been here. There was another telephone in the bedroom, but Colette had been asleep when he left her. Or had she . . .? He turned, walked quickly and silently up the stairs, and threw open the bedroom door.

Three of his bags were on the floor, all open. Colette was on her knees, beside them. She turned and looked up at him with wide, frightened eyes. Around her lay the metal tubes – each one opened – and she had part of the rifle in her hands.

'You were listening,' said the Jackal.

'I . . . wanted to know who you were telephoning each morning like that. This . . . thing; it's a gun, a killer's gun.'

He looked down at her, and for the first time she noticed that his eyes were cold and lifeless. She stood up, dropping the piece of the gun.

'You want to kill him,' she whispered. 'You are one of them – the OAS. You want to use this to kill de Gaulle.'

She tried to run to the door, but he caught her easily and threw her on to the bed. She opened her mouth to shout, but his hand came down hard on the side of her neck, cutting off the sound. He pulled her face down, over the edge of the bed, and hit her again, across the back of the neck, killing her.

He went to the door to listen, but there was no sound from below. Moving quickly, he put the rifle back into the metal tubes and packed it into the bag with the army coat and old clothes of André Martin, and locked it. He then took the clothes of the Danish priest, Per Jensen, from one of the other bags.

He spent the next half-hour washing, cutting and colouring his hair grey. Then he dressed in a black suit, and a priest's shirt and collar, and put the Danish man's passport into his coat pocket. Next he packed the rest of his English clothes in another bag and locked it.

It was nearly eight o'clock when he finished. Soon Ernestine would be coming up with the morning coffee. From the window he watched Louison cycle down the path that led towards the gates. He was going shopping. At that moment, the Jackal heard Ernestine knock on the bedroom door. He made no sound. She knocked again.

'Your coffee, Madame,' she called through the closed door.

'Leave it there,' the Jackal called, making his voice sound sleepy. 'We'll pick it up when we're ready.'

Outside the door, Ernestine was shocked to hear their visitor's voice. Shocked to discover that Madame had taken him to her

'You want to kill him.'

bed. She hurried downstairs to find Louison and tell him, but he had gone.

She did not hear when the bags were dropped slowly from the bedroom window, tied to a sheet. And she did not hear the bedroom door as it was locked from the inside, the dead body of Colette in a sleeping position on the bed with the sheet up to her chin. She did not hear the sound of the bedroom window as it shut behind the grey-haired man who then dropped to the grass below.

She did hear the noise of Colette's car, and saw it drive away from the house. 'Now what is that young lady doing?' she said to herself, as she went back upstairs.

The coffee was still outside the bedroom door. She tried to open the door, but found it was locked. The gentleman's bedroom door was also locked. What was going on? She decided to speak to Louison. He was at the shops, but somebody from the local café would find him.

She did not understand the telephone but she went downstairs, picked it up and listened. Nothing happened. She did not notice that the telephone line had been cut with a knife.

♦

The Jackal threw the bag containing all his English clothes, and the passport of Alexander Duggan, into a river. He drove on to Tulle and parked the car three streets away from the railway station.

At the station, he bought a ticket to Paris and went to wait for the train. A young policeman stopped him and asked to see his papers. The Jackal put down his luggage and took out his Danish passport. The young man looked at it but did not understand a word.

'You are Danish?' he asked in French.

The Jackal seemed not to understand.

'You . . . Danish,' the policeman said, pointing at the passport.

The Jackal smiled, and spoke in Danish. 'Danish. Yes, yes!'

The policeman gave him the passport and moved away to stop another passenger who was coming into the station.

The Paris train was late. It arrived at Tulle at one o'clock. The grey-haired Danish priest took a corner seat, put on a pair of glasses, and began reading a Danish book about French churches. It would be eight o'clock that evening before the train arrived in Paris.

◆

Louison arrived back from the shops at one o'clock and listened to his anxious wife's story.

'I shall get a ladder and look in the window,' he told her.

He did this, and came back five minutes later.

'She is asleep,' he told Ernestine. 'We must not wake her.'

But by four o'clock, the worried Ernestine decided that they must do something, so Louison climbed the ladder again, opened the window and stepped inside. Ernestine watched from below.

After a few minutes the old man's head came out of the window. 'Ernestine,' he called. 'She seems to be dead.'

◆

Lebel heard about Colette's murder at 6.30 that evening. He remembered her name from the hotel guest list at the Hotel du Cerf. Police were now looking for her car, he was told, and the Englishman who was driving it. At 7.30, a policeman in Tulle found the Renault, but it was 8.05 before Lebel got the message from the police at Egletons.

'It was found near the railway station, you say?' said Lebel. He thought for a moment, then asked 'What time will the morning train from Tulle arrive in Paris? Hurry!'

He heard voices talking together at the other end for a

moment, then he got his answer. The morning train from Tulle would arrive in Paris at 8.10 that evening.

Lebel dropped the telephone and ran out of the office, shouting to Caron to follow him.

But they were too late. Their car arrived at the station just as the grey-haired Danish priest was leaving in a taxi.

By nine o'clock Lebel was back in his office, where he received a message to telephone the Tulle police. The young policeman at Tulle railway station had made his report about the passengers who had caught the train to Paris. This information was now passed to Lebel.

Lebel put down the phone five minutes later and turned to Caron. 'We're looking for a Danish priest this time,' he said.

At the progress meeting that evening the Minister and the others in the group listened to Lebel's report about the murder of Colette de la Chalonnière, about the murderer's escape in the Renault, and about the tall, grey-haired Danish priest who caught the Paris train at Tulle.

'So the killer is now in Paris,' Saint-Clair said coldly, when Lebel had finished. 'With a new name and a new face. You have failed once again, Lebel!'

'How many Danes are there in Paris tonight?' asked the Minister.

'Probably several hundred,' said Lebel.

'Can we check them?' said the Minister.

'Only in the morning, when the hotel cards come in.'

The Minister looked round the room. 'There is only one thing I can do now, gentlemen,' he said. 'I must ask the President not to appear anywhere in public until the man is found. And every Dane staying in Paris tonight must be checked first thing in the morning. That is all, gentlemen.'

♦

Lebel spoke to Caron later.

'They think we are stupid and the Jackal is lucky,' he said. 'Well, he's had good luck, but he's also very clever. And we've had bad luck, and we've made mistakes. But twice we've missed him only by hours. First he gets out of Gap with a newly painted car, just in time. Now he kills Colette de la Chalonnière and leaves her house only hours after the Alfa Romeo is found. And each time it's the morning after the progress meeting. Lucien, my friend, I think I'm going to use my powers to listen to some telephone calls.'

Lebel looked out across the River Seine.

Three hundred metres away another man looked out of his window at the summer night. He had grey hair but a young face, and he smoked an English cigarette.

As the two men looked towards each other unknowing across the Seine, the Paris church clocks sounded midnight.

It was now 22nd August.

CHAPTER 9

The Telephone Call

It was 1.30 in the morning when Caron woke Lebel up.

'Chief, I'm sorry about this,' he said, 'but I've had an idea. The Jackal has got a Danish passport, and he almost certainly stole it, yes?'

'Probably,' said Lebel. 'Go on.'

'Well, except for his trip to Paris in July, he has been in London. So he probably stole it in one of those two cities. Now what would a Dane do when his passport was lost or stolen? He'd report it to the representatives of his own government in that city.'

Lebel got out of his bed.

'Sometimes, my dear Lucien, I think you will make a very good detective. Get me Superintendent Thomas at his home in London, then the Danish government representative in Paris.'

He spent another hour on the phone to both men, then went back to bed. At four o'clock he was woken with the message that there were nine hundred and eighty hotel cards filled in by Danes staying in Paris hotels, and that they were being sorted now.

Soon after six o'clock he received another message and immediately took a car and drove with Caron to another small office. Here he listened to a recording of a telephone conversation.

A man's voice said, 'Hello?'

A woman's voice said, 'This is Jacqueline.'

The man's voice said, 'This is Valmy.'

The woman said quickly, 'They know he's a Danish priest. They're checking the hotel cards of all Danes in Paris, and they're going to visit every one.'

There was a pause, then the man's voice said, 'Thank you.' He put down the phone, and the woman did the same.

Lebel thought for a moment, then said, 'Do you know the number she rang?'

'Yes,' said the telephone engineer. 'It was MOLITOR 5901.'

'Do you have the address?'

The man gave him a piece of paper, and Lebel looked at it.

'Come on, Lucien,' he said. 'Let's go and visit Mr Valmy.'

They arrived as Valmy was making himself breakfast. He knew immediately who the four men were when he opened the door. Two were wearing uniforms, and ran towards him. But the short, quiet man stopped them before they reached him. He turned and spoke to Valmy.

'We listened to your telephone calls,' he said softly. 'You're Valmy.'

The other man gave no sign of emotion. He stepped back and let them enter his room. 'Can I get dressed?' he asked.

'Yes, of course,' said Lebel.

He waited behind after they had taken Valmy away and began to look round the room. It was 7.10 when the telephone rang. Lebel watched it for several seconds, then picked it up.

'Hello?' he said.

'It's the Jackal,' said the voice at the other end.

Lebel thought quickly. 'This is Valmy,' he said.

There was a pause, then the voice at the other end said, 'What's new?'

'Nothing,' said Lebel. 'They lost you in Corrèze.' He held his breath. It was important that the man stay where he was for a few hours more. There was a sound, then the telephone was silent. Lebel put it down and ran out to his car.

'Back to the office!' he shouted at the driver.

♦

'This is Valmy.'

The Jackal was worried. Nothing? There must be more than nothing. This detective Lebel was not stupid. They had spoken to the taxi-driver in Egletons, and they had found Colette's body, and the Renault by now. They had questioned the people at the railway station. They had . . .

He went quickly to the hotel desk and spoke to the woman there. 'My bill, please. I am leaving in five minutes.'

◆

The telephone call from Superintendent Thomas came in as Lebel entered his office at 7.30.

'You were right,' Thomas said. 'On 14th July a Danish priest reported that he had lost his passport. He thought it was stolen from his hotel in London, but could not prove it. His name was Per Jensen of Copenhagen, tall, blue eyes, grey hair.'

◆

Four police vehicles arrived outside the hotel on the Quai des Grands Augustins at 8.30. They were too late.

'The priest, Mr Jensen, left an hour ago,' said the manager.

◆

The Jackal took a taxi to the railway station, where he left the bag containing the gun and the army coat and clothes of the imaginary Frenchman, André Martin, in the left-luggage office. He kept the bag with the clothes and papers of the American student, Marty Schulberg. He then got a room at a small hotel round the corner from the station.

Inside his room, the Jackal washed the grey out of his hair, and coloured it brown. He then dressed like an American college boy from New York, including a pair of heavy glasses, and pushed the Danish priest's clothes and passport into a bag.

By the middle of the morning, he was ready to move. The bag

of priest's clothes went into a cupboard, and the cupboard key went down the toilet. He used the fire escape to leave the hotel, so nobody saw him, then took a taxi to the Latin Quarter.*

◆

Superintendent Thomas heard that the French police had missed the Jackal again.

'Now he's in the centre of Paris, and they think he might have another false identity prepared,' he told his men. 'So now we can start asking for a list of passports of visiting foreigners reported lost or stolen since 1st July. Get to work.'

◆

The progress meeting was brought forward to two o'clock in the afternoon. Lebel gave his report quietly, in his usual way.

'The man gets all the luck!' said the Minister.

'No, Minister, it hasn't all been luck,' said Lebel. 'Someone has been informing the Jackal of our progress. This is why he left Gap in a hurry, and why he killed Colette de la Chalonnière and left just before we got there.'

They listened in silence as Lebel went on.

'Every night I've reported my progress to this meeting – and twice he was given that information early the next morning.'

'I seem to remember that you made this suggestion before,' said the Minister. 'I hope you can prove it this time.'

Lebel put a small recording machine on the table and turned it on. They listened to the recorded telephone conversation in silence. Colonel Saint-Clair's face went grey, and his hands were shaking as he collected together the papers in front of him.

'Whose voice was that?' asked the Minister, when the recording had finished.

***

* Latin Quarter: one of the oldest parts of Paris, famous for its universities

Lebel did not speak. Saint-Clair stood up slowly. 'I'm sorry to have to tell you...Minister...that it was the voice of...a friend of mine. She is staying with me. Excuse me.'

He left the room, knowing that he would never be able to work for the President again.

Lebel continued with his report, telling them of his request to Thomas in London for a list of every missing passport over the last fifty days. 'I hope to have names of no more than one or two men who fit the description we already have of the Jackal. As soon as I know, I shall ask for photographs of those people. We can be sure he will by now look more like his new identity than like Calthrop or Duggan or Jensen. With luck, I should have the photographs by midday tomorrow.'

'I must tell you that the President refuses to change his plans to protect himself from this killer,' said the Minister. 'But reporters can now be told that the Jackal is the murderer of Colette de la Chalonnière, if nothing else, and that he is believed to be hiding in Paris. And as soon as you know his new identity, you can give that name and photograph to the newspapers, television and radio reporters. All they will know is that we are looking for a common murderer, nothing else. But every policeman, every security man in Paris will be looking for him. Lebel, all we want from you now is one name, one description, one photograph. After that, we will have the Jackal in six hours.'

'Actually, we have three days,' said Lebel, who had been looking out of the window. His listeners looked surprised.

'How do you know that?' asked the Minister.

'I'm sorry,' said Lebel. 'I've been very silly not to realise it before. For a week now I've been certain that the Jackal has a plan, and that he has chosen his day for killing the President. He knows exactly when he is going to do the job. Minister, has the President any public visits to make today, tomorrow or Saturday?'

'No,' said the Minister.

'And what is Sunday, 25th August?' asked Lebel.

'Of course!' breathed the Minister, 'Liberation Day. And the crazy thing is, most of us were here with him on that day, the Liberation of Paris, 1944.'

'Exactly,' said Lebel. 'The Jackal knows there is one day of the year that General de Gaulle will never spend anywhere except here. It is his great day, and the assassin knows this.'

'Then we have got him,' said the Minister. 'There is no corner of Paris where he can hide. Lebel, get us that man's name.' He looked across at the detective. 'One more thing. Why did you choose Colonel Saint-Clair's telephone to listen to?'

Lebel half-smiled. 'I didn't. We listened to all your telephones last night. Good afternoon, gentlemen.'

♦

It was eight o'clock when Superintendent Thomas telephoned from London with eight names. Carefully he listed them all, with passport numbers and descriptions.

'But three lost their passports when we know the Jackal was not in London,' said Thomas. 'One is too tall — more than two metres. One is extremely fat, and another is too old — more than seventy.'

'What about the last two?' said Lebel.

'One comes from Norway, the other is an American, and both are tall, with wide shoulders. The man from Norway was certain that his passport fell out of his pocket and into the River Thames when he was on a boat with his girlfriend. But the American was sure that his bag, with the passport inside, was stolen at Heathrow Airport. What do you think?'

'Send me all the details of the American, Marty Schulberg,' said Lebel. 'I'll get his photograph from the Passport Office in Washington. And thank you again for all your help.'

♦

There was a second progress meeting that evening at ten o'clock. By then, all those attending had details of Marty Schulberg, wanted for murder. A photograph was expected before morning, in time for the evening papers which would be on the streets at ten o'clock in the morning.

The Minister stood up to speak.

'Gentlemen, when we first met, it was agreed that finding the assassin known as the Jackal was a job for a detective. We were right. Detective Lebel has done a good job, and he has our thanks. But now we have a name, a description, a passport number, and soon we shall have a photograph. I am confident that a few hours after that we shall have our man.' He turned and looked at Lebel. 'So now your job is finished. We can do the rest. Once again, thank you.'

He waited. After a moment, Lebel got up from his seat. He smiled at the others, and they smiled at him. Then he turned and left the room.

For the first time in ten days, Claude Lebel went home to bed. He heard the clock in his house sound midnight.

And it was 23rd August.

CHAPTER 10

The Old Soldier

The Jackal met Jules Bernard in a student bar, soon after midnight. He quickly realised that the young man liked him. After talking together for some time, the student asked him where he was staying.

'I haven't anywhere to stay,' replied the Jackal, speaking like an American. 'I'm a student like you, with no money.'

'Come and stay with me for a few days,' suggested Bernard. He seemed pleased. 'I live alone at the moment.'

They collected the Jackal's two bags from the left-luggage office at the station, then Bernard drove to the place where he lived. It was two small rooms in an old house, but they were clean and comfortable.

During the night, the Jackal checked the food. There was enough for one person for three days, but not enough for two people. They spent the following morning indoors, and at midday they watched the television news. The first report was about the hunt for the killer of Colette de la Chalonnière.

Then a face appeared on the television: a good-looking young face, with brown hair and heavy glasses. It was the killer, said the newsreader. His name was Marty Schulberg, and he was an American student.

A shocked Bernard turned round to look at his new friend. 'The newsreader is wrong,' he said. 'He said that Schulberg's eyes were blue, but your eyes are grey.'

It was the last thing he said. Two hands closed round his neck . . .

A few minutes later, the dead body of Jules Bernard was

A shocked Bernard turned round to look at his new friend.

hanging in a coat cupboard. The Jackal picked up a magazine and prepared to wait for two days.

♦

During those two days Paris was searched as it never had been searched before. Every hotel and guest house was checked. Every bar, restaurant, club and café was visited by secret service men who showed the picture of the wanted man to waiters and barmen. The house or flat of every known friend of the OAS was visited and searched. Hundreds of thousands of men in the streets, in taxis and on buses were stopped and their papers were examined.

On the evening of 24th August Claude Lebel received a telephone call at his home. It was from the Minister, who asked Lebel to come to his private office. A car came for him at six o'clock.

The Minister looked tired and worried. Lebel sat down in a chair opposite him.

'We can't find him,' the Minister said. 'He's disappeared. We are sure that the OAS people don't know where he is either. I don't think we ever really had any idea what kind of man you have been looking for these past two weeks. What do you think?'

'He's here, somewhere,' said Lebel. 'What are the plans for tomorrow? The same?'

'The President won't change anything,' said the Minister. 'A ceremony at the Arc de Triomphe at ten o'clock. Notre Dame at eleven. Then back to the palace for lunch and a short rest. At four o'clock in the afternoon, he will be at a ceremony giving medals to a group of ten old soldiers on the square in front of the Gare de Montparnasse.'★

'What about crowd control?' asked Lebel.

★ Gare de Montparnasse: a railway station in Paris

'They will be kept back further than ever before. Metal security fences will go up several hours before each ceremony. Houses and flats will be searched. There will be watchers with guns on rooftops, looking at the opposite roofs and windows. Nobody gets through the metal fences except those taking part in the ceremonies. And anyone with a package or carrying something long and narrow will be taken away as soon as they are seen. Well, have you any ideas?'

Lebel thought for a moment, then said, 'He will be careful not to get killed himself. He is a professional, he kills for money. He will want to get away and spend it afterwards. He made careful plans when he was here in the last eight days of July, and he knows that every security man will watch for him now that his identity has been discovered. But he won't turn back. Why? Because he thinks he can do it, and get away. He must have some idea that nobody else has ever thought of. A bomb could be discovered, so it must be a rifle. That was why he needed to enter France in a car. The gun was in the car, or probably fixed under it.'

'But he can't get a gun near de Gaulle!' cried the Minister. 'Nobody can get near him, except a few, and they are being searched. How can he get a gun inside the security fences?'

'I don't know,' said Lebel. 'But he thinks he can, and he hasn't failed yet. He's here. With a gun, in hiding, perhaps with another face and identity card. One thing is certain, Minister. He must come out of hiding tomorrow. Your security plans seem perfect, there's nothing more that I can suggest. So may I just walk round each of the ceremonies and see if I can see him? It's the only thing left to do.'

The Minister had hoped for more than this from the man who was described as the best detective in France. 'Of course,' he said coldly. 'Please do that.'

♦

Sunday, 25th August 1963, was very hot, and police officer Pierre Valremy was bored. His shirt was sticking to his back, he was thirsty and it was time for lunch, which he knew he was going to miss.

He turned and looked back up the Rue de Rennes. The metal security fence he was guarding was one of several across the street, from one building to another, about two hundred and fifty metres up the street from the Place du 18 juin. Another two hundred metres further on was where the ceremony was going to happen.

Three long hours to wait. But people were already beginning to stand along the lines of the fences. Valremy could not understand them. Why wait in this heat for hours to see a crowd of heads three hundred metres away, just because de Gaulle would be in the middle of them somewhere?

There were about two hundred people along the fences when he saw the old man. He was coming slowly down the street, wearing a dirty black hat and a long army coat. There was a row of medals hanging on his chest. Several of the crowd by the fence gave him looks full of pity.

These old men always kept their medals, Valremy thought. Perhaps it was the only thing some of them had left in life. Especially when one of your legs had been shot off. When you needed a metal crutch to support you.

'Can I pass?' the old man asked Valremy.

'Let me have a look at your papers.'

The old soldier took two cards from his coat pocket. Valremy looked at them. André Martin, French citizen, age fifty-three, born in Colmar, Alsace; living in Paris. The other card was for the same man and said that André Martin had lost his leg in the war.

Valremy looked at the photographs on each card. They were of the same man, but taken at different times. He looked up.

'Take off your hat.'

'Can I pass?'

The old man took it off. Valremy compared the face in front of him with those in the photographs. The man in front of him looked sick. His face was grey, and his grey hair was sticking up. Valremy gave him back the cards.

'What do you want to go down there for?' he asked.

'I live there,' said the old man. 'I have a room.'

Valremy took the cards back again. The identity card gave the old man's address as 154, Rue de Rennes, Paris, which was further down the road. All right, thought Valremy, there were no orders against letting an old man go home.

'Pass through,' he told the old man. 'But behave yourself. The President will be here in an hour or two.'

The old man smiled and put away his cards, almost dropping his crutch. 'I know,' he said.

The last Valremy saw of the old soldier was the back of the army coat going into a doorway at the far end of the street, next to the square.

Madame Berthe looked up as the shadow fell over her. It had been a tiring day, with policemen looking in all the rooms. Fortunately, all except three of the people living in the house were away on holiday.

'Excuse me,' the man was saying. 'Could I have a glass of water? It is very hot waiting for the ceremony...'

She looked at the old man, who was wearing a long army coat with medals on his chest. He had one leg, and was resting on his crutch. He looked tired and hot.

'Of course!' said Madame Berthe. 'Walking around in this heat – and the ceremony is not for two hours. Come in!'

She walked away into her little room to get a glass of water. The old soldier followed her. She did not hear him close the outside door, and the crash of his hand on the right side of her head behind the ear was quite unexpected. She fell without a sound to the floor.

The Jackal opened the front of his coat and reached inside to untie the piece of leather which held up his right leg. He spent several minutes allowing the blood to run back into the lower half of the leg before standing on it. Five minutes later Madame Berthe was tied up, with a piece of cloth tied across her mouth. He put her in the kitchen and shut the door.

Moments later, he found the keys of the flats in a table drawer. He put them in his pocket. Now he picked up the crutch – the same one which he had used to get through the airports of Brussels and Milan twelve days earlier – and looked out into the hall. It was empty.

The Jackal moved quickly up the stairs to the sixth floor. He chose the flat of Madame Beranger and listened at the door. Silence. He used a key to get inside, closing the door behind him.

He went to the window and looked out. Across the road, on the rooftops of the houses opposite, men in blue uniforms were moving into position. He was only just in time. He opened the window quietly and stepped back.

Keeping in the shadows of the room, he looked down on to the place where de Gaulle was going to stand, a hundred and thirty metres away. He moved a table to one side of the window. Later, he would rest his gun on this.

The crutch came to pieces easily. Lovingly and carefully, the Jackal put the rifle together. Then he lit a cigarette and sat down to wait.

CHAPTER 11

A Question of Identity

Claude Lebel arrived at the Rue de Rennes and looked at his watch. General de Gaulle was on his way now. Lebel moved through the crowd and spoke to policemen.

'See anyone?'

'No, sir.'

'Has anyone been past, anyone at all?'

'No, sir. Not this way.'

He heard someone shout an order down in the square, and from one end of the Boulevard de Montparnasse the black cars swept into the Place du 18 juin. All eyes turned to look at the cars, and the crowd moved forward to get a better view.

Lebel looked up at the rooftops. The watchers there were busy looking at the rooftops and windows across the road, watching for anything that moved.

He reached the western side of the Rue de Rennes.

'Has anyone passed this way?' he asked the young policeman at the security fence there, showing him his detective's card.

'No, sir,' said the young man.

'How long have you been here?'

'Since twelve o'clock, sir, when the street was closed.'

'And nobody has been through?'

'No, sir. Well . . . only an old man, and he lives down there.'

'What old man?' asked Lebel.

'He looked ill, sir. He had his identity card, and the address was 154, Rue de Rennes. I had to let him through, sir. He was hurt in the war and he looked very sick. He was wearing a long, army coat. In this weather! Stupid, really.'

'A long coat?' said Lebel.

'Yes, sir.'

'You say he was hurt in the war. What was wrong with him?'

'He had only one leg, sir. He was walking with a crutch.'

'Crutch?' said Lebel.

'Yes, sir. A crutch. A metal crutch . . .'

Lebel was already running down the street, shouting at the young policeman to follow him.

◆

The Jackal could see the line of old soldiers in the square. He chose the man nearest to him, who would be the first to get his medal, and aimed his rifle at him. In a few moments, facing this man, would be another, taller man.

The security men around one of the cars in the square moved back. From the middle of them came a single tall man. Charles de Gaulle marched towards the old soldiers, alone.

◆

'This one?' said Lebel.

'I think so, sir. Yes, this was the house.'

Lebel ran inside. Moments later, he found Madame Berthe, tied up in the kitchen.

'Top floor!' shouted Lebel, and ran up the stairs with a speed that surprised Valremy, who hurried after him, pulling out his small machine gun as he ran.

◆

The President of France paused at the start of the line of old soldiers. He took the medal from the Minister standing beside him and fixed it to the chest of the old man in front of him. Then he stepped back for the salute.

Six floors up and one hundred and thirty metres away the Jackal held the rifle still and looked down. He could see de Gaulle's face clearly. Softly, gently, his finger moved – and he fired the gun . . .

Half a second later he was looking down at the square, unable to believe his eyes. Before the bullet had passed out of the end of the rifle, the President of France had moved forward again. As the assassin watched, he kissed each cheek of the old man in front of him. Because he was taller, the President had had to bend forward and down to give the traditional kiss after the salute.

It was later agreed that the bullet had passed only a centimetre or two behind the moving head and landed in the road. The President gave no sign that he had heard the shot. The Minister heard nothing, and neither did those people fifty metres away. The silencer on the gun had done its job.

The Jackal was angry. He opened the rifle and pushed in another bullet for a second shot.

◆

Claude Lebel arrived on the sixth floor. There were two doors leading towards the front of the building. He looked from one to the other as the young policeman joined him, his gun ready. Then Lebel heard a soft sound come from behind one of them, and pointed at the door lock.

'Shoot it off,' he ordered, and stood back.

The policeman fired his machine gun, and bits of wood and metal flew in all directions. The door opened into the room. Valremy was first to go in, Lebel behind him.

Valremy recognised the grey hair, but that was all. The man had two legs now, the army coat was gone, and the arms that held the rifle were the arms of a strong young man.

The killer gave him no time. He got up from his seat behind the table and fired the rifle in one smooth movement. The single

'The Jackal.'

bullet made no sound, but there was an explosion in the policeman's chest, killing him. He fell to the floor.

Above his body Claude Lebel looked into the eyes of the other man. 'The Jackal,' he said calmly.

'Lebel,' said the other man. He was already picking up another bullet from the table and pushing it into the rifle.

'He's going to shoot me,' Lebel thought. It didn't seem real. 'He's going to kill me.'

Lebel dropped to his knees and picked up the policeman's machine gun . . .

And fired it.

The noise filled the room. Bullets hit the Jackal in the chest, picked him up, half-turned him in the air, and crashed his body into the corner.

♦

Superintendent Thomas received a telephone call at six o'clock that evening from Paris. Soon after, he spoke to one of his officers.

'They got him,' he said. 'In Paris. No problems, but I'd like you to go to his flat and sort things out.'

It was eight o'clock, when the officer was having a last look at Calthrop's things, that he heard someone come into the flat. He turned. A man was standing there. A big man, who looked annoyed.

'What are you doing here?' asked the police officer.

'I was going to ask you the same thing,' said the man.

'All right, what's your name?'

'Calthrop,' said the man. 'Charles Calthrop. And this is my flat. What are you doing here?'

The police questioned Charles Calthrop for several hours, but had to let him go when three separate reports came through from Paris saying that the Jackal was definitely dead. Also the managers of five hotels in Scotland had said that Charles Calthrop had spent the last three weeks enjoying his holiday, climbing mountains and fishing, and had stayed at their hotels.

'So if the Jackal wasn't Calthrop,' Superintendent Thomas said later, 'then who exactly was he?'

♦

The next day the body of a man was placed in the ground near a small church just outside Paris. The death certificate said that he was an unnamed foreign tourist, killed in a road accident outside the city on Sunday, 25th August 1963. A priest and a policeman took part in the short ceremony.

There was also another man there who did not give his name. A small, quiet man who, when it was finished, turned and walked down the path, to return home to his wife and children.

The day of the Jackal had ended.

ACTIVITIES

Chapter 1

Before you read

1 Read the Introduction. Have you seen the film, *The Day of the Jackal*? What do you know about the French leader, Charles de Gaulle? Have you read any other books by Frederick Forsyth?

2 Look at the Word List at the back of the book.
   a Find new words in your dictionary.
   b Check the meanings of the words below.
      announce   certificate   colonel   crutch   file   forge
      medal   plaster   priest   superintendent   wig
      1) Find three words for people's jobs.
      2) Find two things that you may need if you break your leg.
      3) Find two things made of paper.
      4) Find two things that people wear.
      5) Find two verbs.

3 When the story begins, someone is trying to assassinate the president of France. Discuss these questions.
   a Is the job of president more dangerous in some countries than in others?
   b Do the dangers stop people from trying to become president?
   c Can you name any presidents who have been assassinated?

While you read

4 Answer these questions. Who:
   a is in the car with President de Gaulle?   ....
   b fail to kill the president?   ....
   c is caught by the police?   ....
   d hides behind a curtain in the Hotel Kleist? ....
   e is chief of operations of the OAS?   ....
   f wants half a million dollars as payment
     for a job?   ....
   g lose their passports in London?   ....

100

5 Answer these questions.

    a Why don't Bastien-Thiry's men see the sign for them to shoot?

    b Who are Montclair and Casson?

    c Why does Rodin suggest that the assassin should be a foreigner?

    d Why does the Jackal think it will be especially difficult to escape after killing de Gaulle?

    e Why are banks and jewellers' shops all over France robbed in July?

    f How does the Jackal get a passport in the name of Alexander Duggan?

Chapter 2

Before you read

6 The Jackal is going to Brussels because he wants to buy some things. Which of these do you think he will need?

a bomb   a camera   a false driving certificate   a flat
a French identity card   a haircut   a handgun   a radio
a rifle   a suitcase   an aeroplane   false passports

While you read

7 Complete these sentences with the best ending below.

    a The rifle will be difficult to make because …   .....

    b The rifle will have no number or mark because …   .....

    c The Jackal wears a grey wig for a photograph because …   .....

    d Colonel Rolland is interested in Sandor Kovacs because …   .....

    e The Jackal walks around the famous places in Paris because …   .....

    f The Jackal waits in the square until four o'clock in the afternoon because …   .....

    g The Jackal goes into the Rue Littre because …   .....

    1) … he wants to decide where to kill the president.

    2) … the passport belongs to an older man.

3) … Goossens only has a small workshop.

4) … he had worked with Viktor Kowalski.

5) … he wants to find a way to escape.

6) … Goossens doesn't want to be connected with it.

7) … he expects to kill the president at that time.

After you read

8 The Jackal has to get his rifle past the French police. He wants it to look like something different. We know that this other thing has a shoulder-rest. What do you think it is? Discuss your ideas with another student.

Chapter 3

Before you read

9 Colonel Rolland is going to write a letter.

    a Who to, do you think?

    b With what purpose?

While you read

10 Are these sentences right (✓) or wrong (✗)?

    a Viktor Kowalski's daughter Sylvie is very ill. .....

    b Sylvie isn't living with her real mother. .....

    c The Jackal is pleased with Goossens's work. .....

    d Goossens hopes to have the job finished in two or three days. .....

    e The forger has made cards with three different names on them. .....

    f The Jackal opens the large box because he is looking for his driving certificate. .....

    g JoJo tells Viktor that Sylvie is going to die. .....

After you read

11 Work with a partner. Act out the conversation between the Jackal and the forger, from the moment they arrive in the photographer's shop.

Chapter 4

Before you read

12 The French police are waiting for Viktor Kowalski in Marseilles. They want to catch him and ask him questions. But Kowalski is a very strong man. He knows how to fight and he may have a gun. Where and how do you think the police will catch him?

While you read

13 Put these sentences in the right order. Write the numbers 1–8.

a Colonel Saint-Clair makes a promise. .....

b Roger Frey calls a meeting. .....

c Jacqueline makes a phone call. .....

d Viktor Kowalski shoots a man. .....

e The Jackal flies to Milan. .....

f Colonel Rolland reads a report. .....

g Claude Lebel goes to his office. .....

h The president hears about the Jackal. .....

After you read

14 After Colonel Saint-Clair falls asleep, Jacqueline phones a man called Valmy. She tells him everything that the Colonel has told him about the OAS and their plan to kill the president. With another student, act out their conversation.

Chapters 5–6

Before you read

15 Which of these do you think will happen in these chapters? Discuss your ideas with another student.

a The British police will discover who the Jackal is.

b Colonel Saint-Clair will lose his job.

c The Jackal will rent a garage in Milan.

d The Jackal will fly from Milan to Paris.

e The Jackal will telephone Valmy.

f The British police will learn about the false Duggan passport.

g Lebel will learn that the Jackal is in France.

While you read

16 Who is speaking?
- **a** 'This man … did he have a name?' ....
- **b** 'Did you get Valmy at the post office?' ....
- **c** 'These are stupid mistakes!' ....
- **d** 'I found a copy of the report we were talking about.' ....
- **e** 'Of course he had to get out.' ....
- **f** 'I'm on holiday.' ....
- **g** 'We've been trying to find you for two days!' ....
- **h** 'What do we do now?' ....

After you read

17 Bryn Thomas and Barrie Lloyd are old friends. Their names are typical of one part of the United Kingdom. Use the Internet or a library and find out which part.

Chapter 7

Before you read

18 The Jackal wants to get to know the woman in the hotel. She is beautiful, but perhaps he has another reason. Think about the Jackal's situation. Why might he want to become friendly with her? Discuss your ideas with another student.

While you read

19 Match the events and the dates.
- **a** He arrives in Haute Chalonnière.   22nd July
- **b** He travels from Brussels to Paris.   22nd–30th July
- **c** A man finds the blue Alfa Romeo   31st July
  in a forest.
- **d** He stays in a small hotel in Paris.   16th August
- **e** He travels from Paris to Brussels.   20th August

After you read

20 One word in each sentence is wrong. Change it.

    a Colette sleeps with the Jackal because she feels angry.

    b The Jackal uses the name Calthrop in Paris.

    c The local policeman walks to the Hotel du Cerf.

    d The Jackal leaves the hotel a day later than he expected.

    e The police are looking for a blue Alfa Romeo.

    f The farmer thinks that the Jackal is in the police.

    g The Jackal buys coffee for some farm workers.

    h Colette sees a photograph of her brother in a magazine.

    i Lebel knows that the Jackal is getting money from Paris.

Chapters 8–9

Before you read

21 Lebel thinks that someone at the progress meetings is giving information to someone else. He wants to find out who it is. How can he do this?

22 This chapter's title is 'Another killing'. Who do you think will be killed, and why?

While you read

23 Who is it? Write the names of the people in *italics*.

    a *He* tells the Jackal that the police have found the car. ....

    b *She* thinks that Colette has driven away. ....

    c *He* steals Colette's car. ....

    d *He* discovers that Colette is dead. ....

    e *He* asks about a train time. ....

    f *He* has a good idea and tells *his* boss about it. ....

    g *His* passport was stolen. ....

    h *He* knows that *he* will lose his job. ....

    i *He* gives Lebel information about a student. ....

24 After he leaves the meeting, Colonel Saint-Clair wants to speak to Jacqueline. She is at the police station but they allow him to see her. With another student, act out their conversation.

Chapters 10–11

Before you read

25 Discuss these questions with another student.

    a The Jackal is in Paris but he can't stay in a hotel because the police check all the guests. Where can he stay?

    b How will the Jackal get his rifle past all the bodyguards who are always around the president?

    c How do you think the story will end?

While you read

26 Write short answers to these questions.

    a How does Jules Bernard discover that the police are looking for his new friend?

    ....

    b How does Lebel know that the Jackal will use a rifle?

    ....

    c Why is the 'old man' wearing medals on this day?

    ....

    d How do we know that Madame Berthe isn't dead?

    ....

    e Why does Lebel start running when he hears the words, 'A metal crutch.'?

    ....

    f Why does the Jackal's first bullet miss the president?

    ....

    g Why does Lebel kill the Jackal instead of catching him?

    ....

After you read

27 Who is talking? Who to?

    a 'I'm a student like you …'

    b 'The newsreader is wrong.'

    c 'We can't find him. He's disappeared.'

    d 'He's here. With a gun, in hiding …'

    e 'I live there. I have a room.'

    f '… the ceremony is not for two hours. Come in!'

    g '… only an old man, and he lives down there.'

    h 'They got him.'

    i 'What are you doing here?'

28 Look back at the pictures in the book and discuss these questions with another student.

    a What has happened just before this scene?

    b What is happening in the picture?

    c What is going to happen next?

29 At the end of the story, we still do not know the real identity of the Jackal. Do you think that this is a good ending? Why (not)?

Writing

30 Imagine a meeting between Marc Rodin, René Montclair and André Casson after they have learned that the Jackal has failed to kill the president. Write the conversation between the three of them.

31 Paul Goossens knows that his rifle will be used to kill someone. Do you think it is right for people to make guns? Write your ideas.

32 Read the description of Kovacs's letter to Viktor Kowalski on page 20. Add some more details and write the letter.

33 Lebel has telephone conversations with the chiefs of police in the United States, Britain, Belgium, Holland, Italy, West Germany and South Africa. What does he tell them and what does he want? Write one of these conversations.

34 After the progress meeting in Chapter 5 Lebel's boss, Maurice Bouvier, wants to know what is happening. What does Lebel tell him?

35 After she leaves the Hotel du Cerf, Colette drives home. Later that day, she writes in her diary about the night before. She describes her feelings about her marriage and her reasons for sleeping with 'Alex'. Write her description.

36 Sunday 25th August is Liberation Day. Why does it have this name? Use the Internet or a library to find out and write a report.

37 Imagine that you are the real Charles Calthrop. Write a letter from your London flat to the friend that you went fishing with. Tell the friend what happened when you returned to London.

38 Write Lebel's notes of daily events during his hunt for the Jackal. Start like this: *11th August – My new job is to find an assassin...*

39 Which character in the story do you admire most? Which do you admire least? Give reasons for your opinions.

WORD LIST

announce (v) to tell people about something publicly or officially

assassin (n) a person who murders (**assassinates**) someone for political reasons

(bank) account (n) an arrangement that allows you to keep your money in a bank and take it out when you need it

ceremony (n) a formal event

certificate (n) an official document stating that facts are true or that you have permission to do something

cheek (n) one of the two soft, round parts of your face, below your eyes

colonel (n) an officer with an important position in an army or air force

crutch (n) a special stick with a piece that fits under your arm to help you walk after you have hurt your leg

file (n) a collection of papers about a subject

forge (v) to copy documents illegally so people believe that they are real

gun battle (n) a gunfight between two or more groups of people

identity (n) who you are; an **identity card** has a name, photograph and other information about a person on it

jackal (n) a wild animal like a dog that usually hunts alone, at night, and can run very fast for a long time

liberation (n) the activity of becoming free from control by another country

locker (n) a small cupboard which can be locked, usually in a public places like a railway station

medal (n) a flat piece of metal given to a soldier for his or her bravery

melon (n) a large, round fruit with a hard yellow, orange or green skin and a lot of flat seeds

negative (n) the picture that you produce before you print a photograph; a *negative* is dark in places where the final photograph is light

plaster (n) something white that doctors use to protect a broken leg or arm; it forms a hard case after it dries

priest (n) a church official, with duties and responsibilities in a church or other religious place

pronounce (v) to make the sound of a letter or word

representative (n) someone who acts for another person or group of people

rifle (n) a long gun that you hold against your shoulder before shooting

row (n) a number of things in a line

salute (n) a sign that soldiers use with their officers; they lift their right hand and place it against the side of their head

security (n) ways of keeping people and places safe from attack and other dangers

superintendent (n) an important British police officer

variety (n) a number of people or things of different types

wig (n) false hair that you wear on your head

workshop (n) a room or building with tools in it, where things are made or repaired

The Client
John Grisham

Mark Sway is eleven and he knows a terrible secret. He knows where a body is hidden. Some secrets are so dangerous that it's better not to tell. But it's just as dangerous if you don't. So Mark needs help fast … because there isn't much time.

Seven
Anthony Bruno

Detective Somerset has seven days before he can retire from work and escape from the city. Detective Mills is starting his first week on the job. This story is about seven days and seven shocking murders. The serial killer has one thing on his mind – seven deadly sins.

Strangers on a Train
Patricia Highsmith

"You murder my father and I'll murder your wife."

After Guy Haines meets Charley Bruno on a train he tries to forget about Bruno's plan for the perfect murder. But from this moment Guy is pulled into a world of madness, lies and death – and there is no escape.

There are hundreds of Penguin Readers to choose from – world classics, film adaptations, modern-day crime and adventure, short stories, biographies, American classics, non-fiction, plays …

For a complete list of all Penguin Readers titles, please contact your local Pearson Longman office or visit our website.

Longman Dictionaries

Express yourself with confidence!

*Longman has led the way in ELT dictionaries since 1935.
We constantly talk to students and teachers around the
world to find out what they need from a learner's dictionary.*

Why choose a Longman dictionary?

Easy to understand

Longman invented the Defining Vocabulary – 2000 of the most
common words which are used to write the definitions in our
dictionaries. So Longman definitions are always clear and easy
to understand.

Real, natural English

All Longman dictionaries contain natural examples taken from
real-life that help explain the meaning of a word and show you
how to use it in context.

Avoid common mistakes

Longman dictionaries are written specially for learners, and we
make sure that you get all the help you need to avoid common
mistakes. We analyse typical learners' mistakes and include
notes on how to avoid them.

Innovative CD-ROMs

Longman are leaders in dictionary CD-ROM innovation. Did
you know that a dictionary CD-ROM includes features to help
improve your pronunciation, help you practice for exams and
improve your writing skills?

**For details of all Longman dictionaries, and to choose
the one that's right for you, visit our website:**

www.longman.com/dictionaries